D1482746

ONCE A RENEGADE

Ben Stillman 6

PETER BRANDVOLD

WOLFPACK
PUBLISHING
— EST 2013 —

WOLFPACK
PUBLISHING
— EST 2013 —

Copyright © 2019 (as revised) Peter Brandvold

Cover photography by Rick Evans Photography

Published in the United States by Wolfpack Publishing, Las Vegas

Wolfpack Publishing
6032 Wheat Penny Avenue
Las Vegas, NV 89122

wolfpackpublishing.com

Paperback ISBN 978-1-64119-907-0
eBook ISBN 978-1-64119-906-3

Library of Congress Control Number: 2019937898

ONCE A RENEGADE

For my good friend, Ben Pensiero,
remembering the Arizona years.

I sit in the top of the wood, my eyes closed.
Inaction, no falsifying dream
Between my hooked head and hooked feet:
Or in sleep rehearse perfect kills and eat.

—Ted Hughes, "Hawk Roosting"

CHAPTER ONE

TATE MUELLER HAD just dropped a stout chunk of aspen in the back of the lumber dray when a rifle cracked on the knoll behind him. He whipped around, heart pounding, almost losing his balance.

"Damnit, Tommy!" he yelled. "What in the hell are you shootin' at?"

"Rabbit," came the cool reply, followed closely by the sound of a spent shell bolted out of a rifle breech.

Mueller sighed with exasperation. "Will you cut it out? You damn near gave me a heart stroke, all your fool shootin'. What in the hell are you doin' up there, anyway? You should be down here helpin' me and Hoyt load this wood."

Mueller jerked a thumb at the stocky, heavyset man to his left. Hoyt Jackson was stooping to heft another of the logs he and Mueller had sawed from the thirty-foot aspen they'd felled. He'd frozen on his haunches to stare with a vexed expression at the knoll where Tommy Falk stood with his smoking rifle, outlined against the blue Montana sky studded with high, puffy clouds.

"I'm huntin', you old coot," Falk said in that grinning, arrogant way of his. "If I left it up to you two, we'd be eatin' beans and your lousy corn cakes again tonight."

"You can hunt later, you lazy snipe," the stocky Jackson said, his canvas coat flapping open as he carried another log to the wagon. "Right now, we got work to do. If you don't do it, I don't care how many rabbits you shoot, you ain't eatin' nothin'. And you'll be sleepin' in the privy with the snakes."

He dropped the wood in the dray with a bang, dust puffing up from the gray box boards, the two winter-shaggy Percherons jerking in the traces. Glancing at Mueller, Jackson gave a cunning grin.

"Not only that," Mueller said, eyeing the kid still standing on the knoll, and drawing a big knife from his belt sheath. He flicked his thumb across the razor-sharp blade, a villainous light flashing in his gray eyes. "We'll hold you down and cut off those lovely locks you're so friggin' proud about."

"Anyone messes with my hair again," Falk said as he started down the knoll, auburn locks bouncing on his shoulders, "they're gonna get a bullet through the brisket."

"You think you're fast, kid," Mueller said, "but you ain't that fast. In my day, I'da cut you down to size by now, had you talkin' sweet. Hell, you'd be pourin' my coffee mornin's." He smiled at Jackson standing next to him, both older men leaning against the wagon for a badly needed rest.

"The hell I would," Falk said as he stood his rifle

against a rear wheel of the wagon. He lifted his flat-crowned black hat and ran a gloved hand through his beloved mane, flinging it out from his collar. "You were fast, all right, Tate. Fast at playin' grabby-pants in the bunkhouse at night."

Mueller's expression soured, color drawing up out of his scruffy salt-and-pepper beard. He moved toward the kid, wide-bladed knife in his hand, growling, "Why, you little varmint. I'm—"

"Hey, hey," Jackson said, grabbing Mueller's arm with one hand and pointing eastward with the other. "Look there."

Mueller turned to gaze down Jackson's finger, squinting against the golden spring light reflecting off snow patches scattered amidst the bluestem and buffalo grass. About fifty yards away a horse and rider moved down off the stony southern ridge, meandering through the scattered pines and aspens. A pack mule followed on a lead line, lumpy white panniers draped across its back.

"Who in the hell's that?" Tommy Falk asked.

Mueller chuffed dryly, scowling. "Shambeau."

"Who?"

"Louis Shambeau," Jackson said, the antipathy in his scowl matching that of Mueller's. "Half-breed hider. Metis. Part Indian, part French, and probably a whole lot of other things." He stepped forward and cupped his hands around his mouth. "Hey, Louis! Get the hell out of here. This is Bar Seven range now. It ain't open no more." Waving his right arm, he gestured southward. "Go on.

Go home, breed!"

"Where's he live, anyway?" Falk asked.

"Missouri River country, as far as anyone knows," Mueller said.

"Go on!" Jackson yelled. "Get the hell out of here, Louis!"

But the words could have been shouted off the edge of the world, for all the effect they had. The man riding the spotted horse and trailing the mule didn't so much as turn in his saddle.

"Playin' deaf, are ye?" Mueller growled. "He hears ye, Hoyt."

"I know he hears me."

Suddenly two rifle shots exploded behind them. Jackson and Mueller gave a start, ducking and turning to look. Tommy Falk was holding his Winchester in the air and grinning, smoke curling from the barrel.

"Damnit, kid!" Mueller raged.

Lowering the rifle and jacking out the spent shell, Falk said, "Bet he heard that."

Mueller turned his look eastward again, toward the dark, hatted figure of Louis Shambeau slouched in the saddle. The trapper was now looking their way as he rode at the same slow, deliberate pace as before.

"Yeah, you heard that, didn't ye, breed?" Falk whooped, lifting on the toes of his undershot boots, swinging his Winchester in the air.

Shambeau looked toward the men for several more seconds, then turned away as his horse began descending a brushy swale. In a few seconds he was gone.

"Trappin' Whitetail Creek, no doubt," Jackson grouched.

"Why do you boys hate him so much?" Falk asked through his perpetual grin, the light flashing off his large white teeth.

Jackson only glanced at the kid as he turned back to his work. " 'Cause he's a dirty half-breed, that's why. I lost a brother to those red niggers in sixty-two, and another in sixty-four." He spat and leaned over a stout log. "Get your butt over here, kid, and give me a hand!"

When they finished loading the aspen, they decided to have lunch before felling another tree. Tommy Falk took his grub sack and sat on a log in the wagon box. Jackson sat on a stump, spreading his food in his lap. Mueller sat on the ground nearby, legs crossed Indian-style.

They ate leisurely, Jackson and Mueller engaging in desultory conversation, Tommy Falk lost in his own thoughts, looking owly. He didn't like being sent out on woodcutting detail, especially when it meant being away from the ranch headquarters for several days at a time. Besides, woodcutting was beneath him. He was a good horseman, the best on the Bar 7 roll. He should be home breaking that new remuda of broncs Mr. Hendricks had brought in. And at night he should be in Clantick doing the mattress dance with the hurdy-gurdy girls at Serena's Pleasure Palace and Mrs. Lee's place.

Instead, here he was, in the middle of the Two-Bear Mountains, doomed to cut wood all week with two old coots who not only couldn't cook but could bore the hide off a grizzly bear.

"Good Lord, look what he's doin' now," Jackson carped to Mueller, eyeing the kid disdainfully.

Finished earing, Falk was smoking a cigarette with one hand, combing his hair with the other, his hat resting on his left knee.

"Jesus Christ, he's half girl."

"I'd say he's more than half." Jackson laughed, shaking his head.

"Go to hell," Falk said with an air of strained tolerance. "Girls love my hair. I've been diddled more times because of my hair than the two of you could count with your shoes off."

Jackson reached over and tapped Mueller's knee. "Maybe he's got a point, Tate. You know, those girls in the Drovers do seem to fawn over him. Maybe you and me should grow our hair out." Grinning, he removed his hat and ran his hand over his thinning gray pate. "Think I'd look good with hair as long as the kid's?"

They both laughed but stopped abruptly when they saw the kid standing in the wagon and frowning at something in the distance behind them.

"What is it?" Mueller asked.

"It's your buddy again," Falk said.

"Shit!" Jackson groused, standing and moving out away from the aspen copse and casting his gaze westward. The trapper was heading back the way he'd come, climbing the grade toward the stony, pine-studded ridge. "Sure enough. There he is."

"Must of checked his traps down at the Whitetail," Mueller said.

"Cheeky devil," Jackson muttered. "Thinks he can just waltz through here anytime he wants."

"Ain't it government land?" Falk asked. He was enjoying the older men's anger. It was something, anyway.

"This is the Bar Seven range, you stupid snipe," Jackson lashed, swinging an angry look at the kid. "Mr. Hendricks has lease papers on it."

"So what harm's it do—him trappin' on it?"

Neither Tate nor Mueller found reason to answer such a stupid question. They stood watching the half-breed climbing the grade toward the ridge, their jaws set, eyes squinting against the noon sun, muttering angry oaths under their breaths.

At length, when the trapper was only a few yards from the pines and aspens studding the ridge's northern slope, Falk's rifle cracked again. Tate and Mueller jumped.

"What the—? Damnit, kid!"

"What the hell you shootin' at, you crazy snipe?"

But when Jackson turned away from Falk's self-satisfied countenance, he saw for himself what the kid had been shooting at. He'd been shooting at the trapper's pack mule.

And he'd hit it.

The animal was down on its knees, thrashing, trying to regain its legs, its agonized brays caroming on the wind. The trapper had halted his agitated horse and was looking back at the mule. He turned his head toward the three woodcutters. He looked their way for a long time, sitting stiffly in his saddle, keeping his frightened horse from bolting with one hand gripping the bridle reins.

"Jesus Christ, he shot the mule!" Jackson exclaimed.

The kid laughed. "I bet he heard that, too."

Mueller turned to look at the kid. Falk stood on a log in the wagon box, looking toward the trapper and grinning, holding his rifle down low at his side.

"Why, you crazy devil." Mueller chuckled haltingly. "What in the hell... what in the hell you go and do that for?" He chuckled again nervously and swung his gaze back to the fallen mule.

The trapper had dismounted and was tying his fiddle-footed horse to a pine branch. He shucked his rifle from his saddle boot, and Jackson and Mueller got fidgety, their legs springy, ready to seek cover if they had to.

But the trapper only walked back to the mule, knelt down, and inspected the still-thrashing beast. After a while he stood, stepped back, jacked a shell in the rifle's breech, and took aim at the mule's tossing head.

Smoke puffed from the barrel. A half-second later the report reached the woodcutters' ears.

The mule's head went down, its legs still kicking but with less insistence than before. Finally the animal relaxed and lay still.

The trapper spent the next several minutes stripping the panniers from the mule's back and transferring hides from the mule to the horse. There was only so much room on the horse, however, which already had a good-sized stack of hides strapped to its back, behind the saddle. Shambeau ended up leaving most of the panniers with the mule.

When the transfer was complete, he stood at the rear of his mount and stared at the woodcutters, who'd been watching the procedure in bemused, snickering silence. He stood looking their way for half a minute, but it was too far for the woodcutters to see the expression on his face, a dark blur beneath his black stocking cap.

"Serves ye right!" Mueller said at last. "Now get the hell out of here, and don't come back."

"Yeah, ye greasy snipe!" Jackson put in, waving an arm.

Tommy Falk gave a rebel yell, laughing.

Shambeau turned, stepped into a stirrup, and mounted. He rode up the mountain, not glancing back, and disappeared over the ridge.

"Well, I bet that's the last we'll see of him," the kid said proudly, still grinning at the spot on the ridge where the trapper had gone.

"Greasy snipe," Jackson groused.

Mueller chuckled uneasily.

CHAPTER TWO

THE WOODCUTTING CREW chuckled off and on for the rest of the afternoon about the trick the kid had pulled on the Metis trapper. About five-thirty they called it a day, gathered their saws and axes, piled into the wagon with the kid riding on top of the logs, and headed down the mountain to the line shack nestled in a hollow.

The shack was used mostly by line riders, but in recent years woodcutting details from the Bar 7 bunked in it, since it was about halfway between the ranch and the best wood on the range. There was no use going all the way back to the ranch every night—a rough ride across several creek forks and ravines—when they could sleep here, close to the forest.

When the men had unloaded the wood, stacked it neatly under one of the pole arbors built to keep it dry while it seasoned, they hurried inside to whiskey and supper. The kid had shot a fat mule deer buck on the way down the mountain, taking only the hindquarters, and Jackson fried three hefty steaks in bacon grease and butter, adding a splash of whiskey for flavor.

When they finished eating, Jackson and Mueller poured

fresh whiskies and settled into a cribbage game at the rough-hewn table. The kid sat on his cot, back to the wall, smoking a cigarette and taking occasional sips from the tin cup on the floor by his feet.

Suddenly Jackson's face turned red and he leaned over the table as though choking. Squeals of laughter rolled up from his throat, and he slapped the table with his left hand.

"What the hell's so funny?" Mueller asked him.

Jackson jerked his thumb at the kid and shook his head. He lifted his head, his eyes rheumy from both laughter and whiskey, catching his breath. "I hear the shot an' I turn around and there's the kid, that damn rifle o' his smokin' again. Then I turn back around and see that mule"—he lowered his head, laughing again, and slapped the table—"rollin' around in the brush like a big damn fish on a stringer!"

Mueller chuckled around the cigarette stub wedged in the corner of his mouth. He cut his eyes at the kid, who was combing his hair again, sober-faced. "Kid, you got a devil streak in you."

"You don't know the half of it, old man," the kid said evenly, with a bored, tired air. He wished these old farts would forget about the mule. It had been fun, but it was over, for chrissakes. Now Falk wanted to be left alone so he could imagine what the other Bar 7 boys were doing in town right now, which whores they were making time with.

"You just better not try something like that on the

wrong hombre." Mueller shook his head.

The kid looked at him pointedly. "Why not?"

"'Cause the wrong hombre might take exception, twist your horns for you, not to mention put a bullet through your brisket."

"I'd like to know what hombre's gonna do that."

Mueller chuffed wryly and shook his head.

"What if I shot your mule, Mueller?" the kid said stubbornly, his tiger blood quickening. "What would you do about it?"

Mueller looked at him, eyes darkening. "In my day, kid, you talked to me like that, I'd come over there—"

He stopped suddenly when a horse nickered outside.

"What was that?" Jackson asked in a hushed voice.

"It was one of the horses, you old coot," the kid said caustically. "What'd ye think it was?'

Jackson's head was cocked, listening. "What's got 'em riled?"

"Nothin's got 'em riled," the kid said snidely. "They're horses. They nicker once in a while."

Jackson looked at Mueller. Sucking on his quirley, Mueller shrugged.

The kid laughed. "What do you think—ole Louis Shambeau's comin' to twist my horns fer shootin' his mule?" He laughed again and reached for his whiskey cup. "You two are worse than a couple old women."

Another nicker rose above the soft popping of the fire in the stove.

Jackson looked up from the cribbage board at Mueller.

"Think you should check it out?"

"Why in the hell should I check it out?"

The kid cursed angrily and heaved himself up from the cot. "Here—I'll check it out." He opened the cabin door and called into the black night, "Hey, Shambeau, you out there?"

"Kid, close the damn door!" Mueller rasped.

The kid swaggered drunkenly, one hand on the door latch. "Come on out, Louis," the kid squealed. "Come out, come out, wherever you are. Come out so I can kick your half-breed ass for you. You're frightening these old women in here."

"Kid!" Jackson scolded.

Falk turned from the door, closing it behind him. "Well, I guess he ain't out there," he said. "You old women can shut up about it now and let me sleep."

He sat on his cot and kicked his boots off. He lay down, punched his pillow, and drew the blankets up.

Mueller and Jackson listened quietly, but the only sound was the fire in the stove and a mouse gnawing something beneath the floor. Finally Mueller shrugged, and Jackson returned it. They poured fresh whiskies and hunkered over their game. In a few minutes the kid was snoring.

When he and Jackson had finished another game twenty minutes later, Mueller scraped his chair back, stretching and yawning. "Well, I'm gonna go out and shake the dew from my lily."

"Don't let the breed get ye," Jackson cracked.

Mueller snorted and headed for the door. He stepped outside and stopped, listening and watching. The sky was broadly brushed with stars. The horses were still shadows in the hitch-and-rail corral, silver-limned by the moon rising over the peaks. The air was damp-cool, rife with the smell of the pine wafting from the tin stovepipe.

Finally Mueller gave a self-chastising grunt at his apprehension and walked left of the cabin, near a dirty snowdrift peppered with pine needles, and unbuttoned his trousers. He sighed and cut loose, but it took him several minutes of grunting to get a decent stream going. That damn whiskey. Every year it seemed to take him longer and longer to get rid of it.

Behind him a horse blew. Mueller jerked his head up, looking around. The pines were mostly still. A few branches bobbed almost imperceptibly.

He looked behind him, at the cabin, corral, and at the wood stacked beneath the brush arbors. The wagon sat before the corral, the tongue angling downward.

Nothing seemed to be moving. Still, the hair pricked along Mueller's spine, and he tried to hurry his stream, cursing himself for not bringing a gun out here. But if he had, Jackson would've laughed.

Finally he buttoned up and, looking warily around, headed for the cabin. He tripped the latch and opened the door, trying not to breathe too hard. Jackson was stoking the stove with a stick, whiskey cup in one hand. The kid slept, curled on his side. Jackson looked at Mueller.

"Any bogeymen out there?" he asked with a grin.

"Ha-ha."

Mueller swung the door closed behind him. He'd taken two steps toward the table when the door exploded inward, wood casing flying everywhere. Before he could turn around, a man in a buffalo coat bolted into the room, grabbed his hair to steady his head, and ran a wide-bladed knife across his throat.

Mueller didn't even have time to scream. As he dropped to his knees, stunned, blood gushing from his neck, Jackson jumped up from his chair. His face was a mask of horror and surprise. Before he had time to lunge for his gun, the intruder threw his gigantic knife. It careened end over end through the air and landed in Jackson's chest with a *whomp* and a *snap*.

By this time the kid had bolted off his cot, bounding toward the chair over which his gun belt was looped. The intruder lifted an old Colt Navy and fired. The kid screamed and went down howling.

Grabbing a second big knife from his belts, the intruder leaped toward him, grabbed a' handful of his thick auburn hair, and gave a savage pull, yanking the kid's head back. Holding the kid's head with one hand, wielding the knife with the other, the intruder shouted, "You think it's funny to shoot my mule!"

Then, in one clean swipe of the knife, he sliced the kid's scalp from his head and held the bloody mane high in his fist. "I didn't think it was funny! Not at all. But this—I think this is very funny." His laugh was low and throaty.

The kid was screaming, rolling on his back, and holding his head. "My hair! Ah, my God! My *hair!*"

The intruder walked to the door and turned around. He

held the kid's scalp aloft once more, a silver-toothed grin on his big, bearded face. "Now it's my turn to laugh, no?" Then he turned and was gone as fast as he'd come.

***

The sound was like a stout branch snapping far away, but something told Roy Early that it had not been a branch. It had sounded more like a pistol shot.

Early brought his gray mare to a halt on a hillside over the creek he had just crossed and listened, his heart quickening, feeling hopeful. Normally if he were out here alone at night, the sound of a gun would not be a welcome one at all. But tonight Roy Early, who ranched with his brother along Rock Creek east of the town of Big Sandy, had gotten himself lost.

He didn't know how he'd done it, but he'd been chasing a herd of elk late in the day and suddenly ceased recognizing terrain. Then it got dark, and here he was, listening for another shot that might lead him to people who could point him home.

At the moment he wasn't too worried about how friendly they were. He just wanted to get home before his horse played out. Besides, that pistol shot had probably been fired by another hunter like himself, or by some line rider trying to keep a coon away from his grub sack.

When no more shots pierced the cool, quiet night, Early gigged his horse along the mountain, through a sprinkling of pines casting their dark silhouettes against the starry sky and down through an aspen copse. When he came to a game trail, he followed it in what seemed an easterly direction but for all he knew could've been north or even west. There weren't enough stars out yet to get a decent reckoning.

Finally a dull light shone through the trees on his left, and Early, feeling almost giddy with relief, swung the mare off the trail. When he came to the clearing in which the cabin sat, he stopped.

Whores in hell! That was the Bar 7's woodcutting shack, which meant this was Davis Hollow and he was a good six miles and several watersheds from where he'd started out!

Amazed that he could have gotten this lost and relieved to know where he was at last—in spite of having a long ride home through the dark—he spurred his horse ahead. But then he stopped, frowning.

The gunshot.

Wariness creeping in, he called, "Hello the cabin!" His voice was tentative, cautious.

He peered at the hovel through the pine branches, waiting and listening. There were no sounds but the distant calls of night birds and occasional coyotes. He'd ridden up on the cabin's backside, and a single window shed wan yellow light on the half-melted snowdrift below. The window betrayed no movement within.

Puzzled, Early gigged his horse slowly forward, its hooves crunching pinecones and needles. When he came to the window, he ducked his head to peer inside. Instantly he recoiled, gasping.

"My Lord!"

He kneed the horse around the cabin and dismounted, letting the reins drop. Muttering oaths beneath his breath, he ran to the open door and stopped, looking inside with his jaw hanging. He stood there, at once shuddering and sweating inside his wool-lined denim coat, hands away from his sides, fingers twitching.

"Jesus... Jesus God... what the...*hell?*"

Then one of the men inside groaned painfully, gave a clipped cry. Surprised that any of them were alive, least of all the youngest one lying in a pool of his own blood, a grisly red swath where his hair had been, Early kicked a fallen chair away and moved into the cabin.

He knelt beside the kid. The kid's eyes were squeezed shut, but his lips were moving. "Hel... hel-p... *me... please!*"

CHAPTER THREE

BEN STILLMAN AWOKE to soft morning light touching the bedroom window. No frost on the glass nor any ubiquitous icy chill seeping through the sill and up from the floor.

Winter was over.

This far north, only forty miles from the Canadian line, that was a real blessing. Like a second birth, no matter how many times you'd been through it.

"Jesus, I'm getting old," Stillman groused to himself, keeping his voice a whisper.

He remembered hearing his father and his father's friends grouch about the cold and snow back in Pennsylvania and not understanding the aversion. He'd been a boy who loved snowball fights and sleigh rides. He hadn't even minded forking hay all day in the pasture when the temperature stayed well below zero.

Now he understood. And the fact that he did meant he was getting old—as if the salt in his longish brown hair and thick mustache hadn't begun telling him that several years ago, when he'd hit forty.

Okay, so he was middle-aged. Nevertheless, he thought now, his hands laced behind his head, he always felt young when spring hit, melting the drifts along First Street and pushing the first green shoots up through the pastures surrounding the town. His town: Clantick, Montana Territory.

The soft, pinkish opal light made him think of his wife, and he turned to her now, sleeping beside him, her chocolate tresses fanned across her pillow. With his eyes he traced the straight, delicate line of her lovely jaw, caressed her smooth, pale cheeks, the almond shapes of her closed eyes, the resolute nub of her dimpled chin.

An aristocratic chin. Hell, the whole package, right down to her toes, belonged to the French gentry. Her family's name had been Beaumont, and though they'd ranched along the Powder River in Montana, they'd immigrated from France when Fay was a child, and she'd been homeschooled in the French classics and Latin.

Every inch of her bespoke that regal lineage. But Stillman had her now—the middle-aged sheriff of a little one-horse town in the middle of nowhere who hated winter, loved spring, suffered the bullet a drunk parlor girl had lodged in his back several years ago, and tended chickens in the little makeshift coop in his backyard.

He grinned at the thought of his having this lovely young woman in his bed. His wife of three years. This bewitching French princess.

His desire stirred. She seemed to sense it and opened her eyes, the two brown orbs burrowing at him through the misty shadows. Reading his mind, the corners of her full mouth rose slightly.

"I know what you're thinking about, Sheriff." As always, her silky voice betrayed a slight French accent, arousing him further.

"Better not. It's still early, and you need your sleep."

Her eyes burned sensually into his as she slid toward him and lowered her hands through the quilts, finding him. "Are you sure?"

Stillman swallowed as she worked very softly, deftly, gently torturing him with her fingers. "No."

She smiled and sat up, the quilts falling away. Quickly she lifted her nightgown over her head, shaking her thick hair back from her shoulders, exposing her heavy, round breasts. She turned and straddled him, drawing the quilts over her shoulders with one hand.

Then, tightening her thighs against his hips, she leaned down and kissed him, probing his mouth with her tongue. He put his arms around her and held her tightly as they kissed. He balled his fists in her hair and sighed with desire, feeling her squirm against him, flattening her breasts against his chest.

He ran his large hands down her fragile, narrow back to her round bottom, caressing her, enjoying the silky feel of her skin against his own. Then she drew away from his mouth, giving his lower lip an enticing nibble, and kissed her way down his chest and belly, until her hot, wet mouth closed over him and he it was all he could do to keep from screaming.

***

Afterward, they lay talking languidly about the day ahead, and then they made love once more in the traditional way.

When they were through, she held him there, ran her hands through his thick mane. "My ... what's with you this morning?" She gave a luscious laugh.

He smiled and kissed her smooth forehead. "I feel... young today."

"You are young."

"Not in years."

"You're forty-six."

"That's old. On the frontier, that's ancient."

"Well, it's not the frontier anymore. Not really. Haven't you heard about the electric lights they're getting back East? And Crystal told me just the other day about horseless carriages."

Stillman shook his head. "They ain't here yet. No, this is still the frontier, will be for a good while to come. A place where young men get old awful fast."

"Well, I disagree," she said, rubbing his leathery cheeks between her hands and kissing his lips playfully. "And anyway, you're not old. No old man performs the way you just performed, dear heart." She laughed again, lustily.

Stillman sighed and swung out of bed, nude, and walked to the window. He stepped to the side so Mrs. Bennett from next door didn't peek in, as she was wont to do, and have a stroke.

"Doesn't matter," he said dreamily, staring out at the burgeoning dawn. "It's spring, and I feel young." He glanced over his shoulder at Fay. "But then, there's really no excuse for not always feeling young, married to a woman like you."

"Why, thank you, kind Sheriff."

She smiled radiantly, as only Fay could smile, then tossed away the quilts, and swung her coltish legs to the floor. Standing, she grabbed a flannel wrapper off a wall peg. Heading for the door, she said, "I'll get a fire going and put the coffee on. I should get over to the school as soon as I can. More grading to do."

"You assign too many themes," he called to her.

"Don't I know it," she returned from down the hall.

Stillman had washed at the basin and was combing his hair in the mirror over the washstand when he spied movement out the window. Setting down the comb, he peered out. Three men on horseback were trotting down the street, including Stillman's deputy, Leon McMannigle. The other two men Stillman recognized as rancher Walt Hendricks and his foreman, Dave Groom.

Frowning, Stillman watched the three disappear around the house, knowing by the serious expression on his deputy's face they were heading here.

"What now?" Stillman asked himself, reaching for his shirt.

Hendricks had had problems with horse thieves last fall. If he was having them again, Stillman could look forward to three or four days on horseback in the Two-Bear Mountains, where it was no doubt still plenty cold. "Christ."

He grabbed his gun belt and was heading for the living room when someone knocked on the door. "I'll get it," he called to Fay, who met him halfway with a mug of coffee.

He kissed her cheek, accepted the coffee, and opened the door. McMannigle stood on the porch—a rangy, muscular black man with a pleasant face and humorous eyes. His deputy sheriff's star caught the morning light, glowing brightly against his black cowhide vest.

Behind him, Hendricks and Groom sat their horses stiffly. Neither one waved or even acknowledged Stillman with his eyes.

"Mornin'," Stillman said to his deputy.

"Mornin', Ben." Leon's voice was grim, his expression at once wry and ominous.

"Trouble?"

"Yep." The deputy jerked a thumb over his shoulder. "I wanted to come alone and get you, call you over to the jail, but they wanted to tag along. They're a little hot under the collar. Left their ranch about five o'clock this morning."

"Horse thieves?"

"Nope." McMannigle's eyes were round and dark. Stillman could tell he wanted him to get the story from Hendricks himself, which meant it was bigger trouble than he'd suspected.

"Ah, crap." Stillman sighed. "Entertain them a minute, will you?"

"Sure."

Stillman went back in and found his buckskin mackinaw and scarf, which he hadn't worn for a couple weeks but he'd need if he was called into the Two-Bears. Hendricks's ranch was up fairly high. When he'd grabbed his soogan from the closet in the hall, he walked into the kitchen.

Fay turned from the range, a spatula in her hand. She looked at the mackinaw and bedroll in Stillman's arms and winced, knowing it had been trouble at the door. "What is it?"

"I don't know, but Walt Hendricks is out there lookin' like he drank some bad milk. I may be awhile."

"I hope it's not last fall all over again." She was referring to the horse thieves he'd chased for the better part of a week last October, and whom he'd finally caught on the eastern slopes of the Two-Bears with twelve of Hendricks's best peg ponies.

Stillman shook his head and finished his coffee. "Hard to tell."

"Here—eat." Fay was shoveling eggs onto a plate. "I didn't have time to fry bacon."

"No time," he said, and kissed her cheek.

"Ben, you have to eat something!"

He looked at her. Seeing how determined and worried she was, he grabbed a fork and shoveled several loads into his mouth. He washed them down with coffee from Fay's cup and kissed her on that ravishing mouth.

He looked at her seriously. "I'm sorry," he said. "I know it's always something." He meant more than that; he meant he was sorry for bringing her back here from Denver to live as a sheriff's wife and one-room school teacher when she deserved so much more. All that was in his eyes.

She returned his look, smiled, and pinched his cheeks lovingly, bringing her face close to his. "If I've told you once, I've told you a thousand times, I'm happy... as long as you are."

He smiled and kissed her again. "Gotta go. Give those little jaspers hell today."

"Ben, you be careful!" she called as he headed through the living room.

Grabbing his Henry rifle from behind the elk horn rocker, he said, "I love you," and headed outside, his arms so full that he had to fumble with the door to close it behind him.

On the porch he regarded Leon standing with the two mounted men. "I take it I'm gonna need my horse..."

"Yep." Leon nodded.

"I'll meet you around back."

Stillman walked around the house to the old buggy shed, half of which he'd converted into a chicken coop. In the other half, he stabled his bay gelding, Sweets, and Fay's black mare, Dorothy.

He set his coat, soogan, and rifle in the stable, then walked through the adjoining door to feed the chickens he'd wintered over. When he came back to the stable, Leon, Walt Hendricks, and Dave Groom were riding up to the open rear door.

"Come on in," Stillman called above the din of the chickens feeding behind the wood partition. He reached for his saddle. "Fill me in while I leather up."

The three men came into the stable. McMannigle and Dave Groom were smoking. Walt Hendricks was in his early fifties, a stout man with the weathered hide of an aging cowboy. In his crisp denims, string tie, checked shirt, duck coat, and crisp white Stetson, he was all business.

"It's bad, Sheriff," he said, anger flaring behind his sky-blue eyes. "Two of my men were murdered last night in the old line shack they use for woodcutting. Another one was scalped."

Stillman stopped what he was doing to look at Hendricks, surprised. "Scalped?"

"You heard me right. The kid's alive, though. Roy Early found him and brought him back to the ranch. He was shot, too—winged."

"He tell who did it?"

Hendricks stiffened, expressionless. Color moved up his suety face, and his reddish-gray mustache twitched. "Louis Shambeau."

Stillman dropped his saddlebags over his horse's rump and looked at Hendricks again. "The mountain man?"

"That's right."

"Why?"

Hendricks shook his head. "Don't know. The kid was in no condition to go into detail. Lost a lot of blood. You should see his head." The man's head wagged again, his thin-lipped mouth a slash. "The kid had a mop my daughters envied. No more."

"That bad, huh?" Leon asked.

Hendricks made a slashing motion with his right hand,

and whistled.

"The man must've gone nuts," the foreman, Dave Groom, said.

"My men wanted to track him themselves," Hendricks told Stillman. "I gave them orders to stay put. I told 'em trackin' killers is your job. We have calving to worry about."

Stillman poked his Henry down his rifle boot, then grabbed Sweets's reins and backed him out of the stall, sharing a meaningful glance with Leon. "Appreciate that."

"You better find him, though, Sheriff," Hendricks said sharply. "Or my men will."

"Pretty riled, are they?"

"Hell, wouldn't you be?" Groom said, blowing cigarette smoke. "Crazy man out there, runnin' loose in the mountains, butcherin' your pals?'

"The boy need a doctor?" Stillman asked Hendricks.

"I'll say he does."

Stillman told them they'd stop at Evans's place before heading out to the Bar 7.

Groom chuckled dryly. "That horse doctor?"

"You know of anyone else?" Hendricks asked the foreman.

Groom looked at Stillman, then McMannigle. Neither said anything. Groom shrugged.

"Evans's place it is," Stillman said, grabbing his horn and forking leather.

As they rode out, Leon gigged his horse up beside Stillman's. "What do you think?"

Stillman sucked air through his teeth and shook his head.

CHAPTER FOUR

THE TOWN WAS starting to come alive when Stillman and the others trotted their horses down First Street, the smell of bacon wafting from the chimney pipe over Sam Wa's Cafe.

"Sure could use a little food in my gullet," Leon groused. He and Stillman rode side-by-side, Hendricks and his foreman behind them. "They came just as I was about to head to Sam's for breakfast."

"Why don't you head there now?" Stillman said.

The deputy wrinkled his curly black brows. "Huh?"

"It'll give me time to get a pot of coffee into the doctor. You know how he is. His pump usually needs some priming after he's been up drinking most of the night... and what nights hasn't he?"

Leon glanced behind him at the eager-looking Hendricks and his foreman. "What about them?"

Stillman reined his horse to a halt and turned to the rancher and Dave Groom. "Why don't you boys and my deputy here have yourself some breakfast while I fetch the doc?"

He could tell the idea agreed with Dave Groom, who glanced at his boss hopefully. Hendricks set his jaw and wrinkled his nose. "You mean so you can wrestle him out of his stupor? That man's drinking is known throughout the county. That and his lechery."

"He does have a reputation," Stillman allowed.

"Well, tell him we don't have all morning," Hendricks grumbled, reining his horse over to the hitchrack before the café. "My wife and daughters are doctorin' that kid, but he needs a sawbones or he's liable to bleed dry. And my men will only wait so long before they take after that lunatic themselves."

"I'll tell him," Stillman said. He gave McMannigle a mock salute then spurred his horse down the street.

At the west end of town, he turned left onto a wagon trail that climbed a bluff overlooking the town and the Milk River in the north. Dr. Clyde Evans's red, two-story house sat atop the butte, flanked by a woodshed, a buggy shed, a two-hole privy, and a well.

Glancing over the outbuildings, Stillman glanced away and then looked back again. Each was right where it had always been, but the privy no longer sat askew, and someone had repaired the gaping hole in the buggy shed's roof put there when a branch had fallen from the great cottonwood standing over it.

In the stable sitting catty-corner to the house, under a large box elder, Evans's stout gelding poked its head out the top half of the Dutch door. Damn, if the door wasn't sporting a new set of hinges, glistening silver in the climbing morning sun!

"Mornin', Faustus," Stillman said, frowning wonderingly as he dismounted before the unpainted picket fence and looped his reins over the hitching post

"Morning."

Surprised, Stillman whipped his head around. It was Evans himself, in the shaded western side of the house, holding a splitting maul in his hands. He was dressed as always, but his brown dress slacks appeared crisper, his white shirt less wrinkled, his vest less worn, and the brim of the bowler less frayed. A customary stogie poked out from under his bushy red mustache, and his round-rimmed spectacles flashed in the soft morning light.

Stillman blinked. "What the hell are you doin' up this early?"

The doctor, who stood five-ten and reminded Stillman more of an Irish boxer he'd once known in Kansas City than your stereotypical sawbones, brought the splitter down cleanly through a pine log, cleaving it in two. He didn't appear to be drunk, which was also a surprise. The only times Stillman had seen the man awake this time of the day, he hadn't yet been to bed—at least to sleep, and he'd been three or four sheets to the wind.

"Early bird gets the worm."

"When have you ever worried about the worm? I thought I was going to have to flush your blood with some black coffee."

"Already had a pot," Evans said, bringing the splitter down again.

"What's goin' on?" Stillman asked as he pushed through the fence gate.

"What do you mean?"

With a wave of his gloved hand, the sheriff indicated the outbuildings. "Who's been doin' all the work?"

Evans looked around and shrugged. "Me, mostly," he said, arranging another log on the chopping block. "Of course, the Dorfman boy helps a little after school." He shrugged again and plunged the splitter through the pine log. "Just had the urge to straighten up the place a little. When it warms up I'm going to paint the house and the fence and repair that gate there, too."

"Jesus jump," Stillman said, eyeing the doctor, befuddled. Was this the same Clyde Evans he'd gotten to know after moving here from Denver two years ago? The perpetual wisecracking medico with a penchant for whiskey, all-night poker games, and, after so much rye, quoting Shakespearian soliloquies to saloon girls?

"Well, hell, Ben—you're the one's been harpin' on me to get that roof fixed!"

"I know, I know," Stillman said, nodding, "because if you didn't, dry rot would've taken the whole damn building. But I never expected you to take my advice. I mean, it ain't like you ever have before!"

Evans sighed with mock anger and leaned on the handle of his splitter. "If you're done scolding me for my productivity, Sheriff, maybe you'd tell me to what or whom I owe the pleasure of your visit?"

"One of Walt Hendricks's boys is in a bad way. He was

scalped last night."

Evans frowned and regarded Stillman skeptically. "Scalped?"

"According to the kid, Louis Shambeau's the culprit."

"The trapper? What'd he do, go nuts livin' out there all by himself?"

"That's what I'm going to find out. We need you to tend the kid. Leon, Hendricks, and his foreman are waiting for us at Sam Wa's."

"All right, all right" Evans groused, squatting to gather the logs he'd split. "Let me get this wood inside, and I'll grab my bag."

Stillman stooped to gather a load himself then followed the doctor through the porch and into the house where the smell of breakfast rode the air warmed by the big iron range. A woman stood at the stove, and when she turned and saw Stillman, she gave a startled cry and jumped back, slapping her chest with her left hand. In her right she clutched the spatula she'd been scrambling eggs with.

"Oh! Sheriff... good morning...."

Stillman stopped in the entry, wondering when all the surprises were going to cease. The woman standing before him—tall and severe and plainly dressed, but pretty if you looked close, with chestnut hair coiled in a taut bun—was none other than Mrs. Katherine Kemmett, widow of Angus Kemmett, the Lutheran minister who died of a brain hemorrhage two years ago.

Stillman nodded, smiling and sliding his eyes toward the doctor, who dropped his load of wood in the box beside the range. "Mornin', Mrs. Kemmett. Sorry if I frightened you."

"Oh, you didn't frighten me as much as startled me," she said a little breathless, self-consciously smoothing her apron against her dress.

"Well, I'm sorry I startled you, then," Stillman said as he dropped his wood in the box.

Mrs. Kemmett was back stirring the eggs, but a flush remained high in her cheeks. "I'm sure this looks a little strange"—she smiled ruefully—"me being here at this hour. I just... I just want to assure you, Sheriff, that nothing inappropriate has occurred."

The doctor had disappeared, but his footsteps could be heard as he gathered his things in the little room which served as his office and examining room.

To Mrs. Kemmett, Stillman said, "Oh, I didn't think—"

"I mean," she interrupted, "I certainly didn't stay ... I certainly wasn't here last night.... I just came over this morning."

"Of course," Stillman assured her.

"I just came over this morning to fix Clyde's—I mean Dr. Evans's—breakfast. He wouldn't eat a thing if I didn't take matters into my own hands."

"No, he wouldn't," Stillman agreed, his gaze straying around the kitchen, noting that the books which normally littered the small wood table were not only diminished in number but were neatly stacked against the wall. There were no crusted coffee cups or whiskey glasses or uncorked Scotch bottles. The ashtray which usually overflowed with cigarette and cigar butts had been scrubbed clean.

Not only that, but the grease that normally coated every inch of the range was gone!

Noting Stillman's appraisal and no doubt the dumbfounded look on his face, Katherine said, "As you can see, I cleaned up a bit. I mean, I do work here too, Sheriff—as the doctor's assistant and midwife, and that's the reason—the *only* reason—why I did some ... rearranging. I mean, what a horror for the patients!"

The doctor poked his head out of his office. "Katherine, where did you put my wool union suit after you washed it?"

"I hung it in your closet, Clyde."

"Oh." Evans pulled his head back into his office, and Katherine turned to Stillman, blushing girlishly all over again.

Stillman dropped his chin and cleared his throat. "Well, Mrs. Kemmett, you certainly have been doing your duty and then some. I'm sure the good doctor appreciates every bit of your... rearranging." Stillman couldn't fight off the smile tugging his mustache.

He wasn't sure, but he thought he noted a convivial gleam enter those traditionally stoic, cool eyes of Katherine Kemmett—the eyes of a pious minister's wife. She busied herself by shoveling eggs and bacon between the buttered halves of several biscuits.

"These are for you and Clyde," she said neutrally, wrapping the biscuits in paper. "I take it he's needed somewhere this morning?"

"Yes, ma'am—out at the Hendricks ranch, as a matter of fact." Feeling the need to hurry as well as wanting to avoid having to share the grisly details with her, he said, "You know, I think I'll go out and saddle ole Faustus for the doctor so we can get a move on. Let him know where I am, will you, Mrs. Kemmett?" He raised his hat to her as he backed onto the porch. "And I thank you mighty kindly for the biscuits."

"You're most welcome, Sheriff," she said, smiling. Stillman noticed that she not only seemed lighter of mood and demeanor, but she appeared more youthful as well. Always in the past, she had looked and acted at least ten years older than her thirty-some years. "And please, Sheriff," she added, regarding him directly, her eyes flashing, "please call me Katherine."

Taken off guard, Stillman hesitated a moment, then nodded, returning her smile. "I will do that, ma'am—Katherine. Good morning to you, and thanks again." With that he pulled the door closed and strode across the porch, shaking his head.

He'd bridled and saddled Faustus and was leading the horse outside as Evans walked from the house. Seeing Stillman's grin, Evans scowled, nettled. "What?"

"I see what's happening, Doc." Stillman handed the man his reins and headed for his own horse.

"What are you talking about?" Evans said defensively, climbing into his saddle.

Doing likewise, Stillman said, "You're sweet on Mrs.

Kemmett. It sure as hell is obvious she's sweet on you."

"Again, Sheriff, I have no idea what you're talking about."

They were riding out of the yard, their horses snorting, hooves thumping on the trail still damp with snowmelt, spring birds chattering in the brush. Below the butte, a train whistle blew.

"The work you're doin' on your buildings, your new duds"—Stillman grinned at him—"why, Clyde, I'd say you're head over heels in love with that gal!"

"Oh, hogwash," Evans grumbled. "It's a business relationship. She cleans the house and keeps me sober so I don't horrify our patients."

"Call it what you want."

"But you know," Evans said, suddenly wistful, "I have always had the urge, however ignoble, to make a preacher's wife sing—if you, uh, know what I mean." Evans grinned.

Stillman chuckled in spite of himself, shaking his head. "You can fool yourself, Clyde, but you can't fool me. It's more than loin fever that's got you acting almost human." Descending the butte, he swung his horse eastward down First Street. "Come on. We'd better get over to the cafe and rescue Leon from the Bar Seven boys."

CHAPTER FIVE

DURING THE RIDE out to the Bar 7, Stillman grilled Hendricks and his foreman for more details about the killings and scalping, but neither man could offer anything more than what they'd already told him: Louis Shambeau had attacked the three in their cabin, killing two lifelong ranch hands named Jackson and Mueller and savagely removing the hair and scalp of a kid named Falk. At least the crown of it, leaving the sides and a little in back.

Since there wasn't much to discuss, it was a fairly quiet ride. The doctor, knowing he was neither respected nor liked by the two Bar 7 men, quoted lines of Homer and Dante Alighieri, evoking even more of their scorn and completely ignoring it, to their total frustration.

"What the hell language is he speaking, anyway?" Tie foreman asked Stillman.

"The language of love and of the horrors of human mortality, friend," Evans said, riding last in the group, old Faustus plodding along. "Certainly, you must have heard it, lying awake late at night in the darkness of the bunk-house or out under the stars with the wolves howling and the spirits of the cosmos chanting your name?"

Riding up beside Stillman, Leon shook his head and snickered.

Dave Groom peered over his shoulder at the medico, looking as though he'd eaten something rancid. "Jesus God, he's strange!"

"He'd love you to think so, anyway." Stillman chuckled.

They approached the ranch nestled in a high hanging valley a half hour later. Here the air was noticeably colder, and all the men donned coats. Snow lingered in the pines carpeting the north-facing slopes.

Hendricks passed through the main gate. Stillman and the others followed him to the two-story lodge where three women stood on the gallery in shawls, arms folded across their chests as if chilled.

Stillman saw a handful of men lingering in the main corral, bunched and talking amongst themselves, several sitting on the corral fence, heels hooked over the slats. Smoking and sipping coffee from steaming cups, they all turned to watch the newcomers pull their mounts up to the house.

"Ida, where's the boy?" Hendricks asked his wife, a stout, dark-haired woman in a shapeless calico dress.

Stillman took the two girls standing beside her to be their daughters. Both appeared in their teens with pinched faces, dull eyes, and lackluster hair—one blond like her father, the other dark like her mother.

"He's in the bunkhouse," Mrs. Hendricks said, nodding at the long, low structure on the other side of a meandering creek, just south of the corrals. "I tried to get him up here to the house where we could doctor him, but he wouldn't come. Said he didn't want anyone seein' him."

"Well, he's probably bled to death by now!" Hendricks said, admonishing his wife.

"Well, what did you want me to do about it, Walt?" the woman brusquely retorted, eyes afire. "If he wouldn't come, he wouldn't come. The men tried to bring him, and he pulled a gun on them! That's why they're all gathered in die corral like cattle."

Hendricks glanced at Stillman and shrugged.

Stillman turned to Evans and McMannigle. "Well, let's go see what we can do, Doc." As he turned his horse toward the bunkhouse, Leon and Evans following, Stillman turned back to Mrs. Hendricks. "Where are the dead men, Mrs. Hendricks?"

"The boys laid them out in the blacksmith shop, in their coffins. They're ready to be buried as soon as you're done with them." The woman's voice grew stern. "Then maybe we can all get back to work around here." She hit Dave Groom and her husband with a visual lance, then wheeled and headed into the cabin.

Stillman glanced at Hendricks, who only shrugged and raised his hands, palm up.

"And people ask why I never married," Evans muttered as he followed the sheriff and McMannigle onto the log bridge traversing the creek.

The three men reined up before the bunkhouse. Mc-Mannigle said he'd check out the two dead men while Stillman and Evans tended the kid. He kneed his horse toward the blacksmith shop.

Stillman and Evans dismounted their horses and looped their reins over the tie rack.

"I better check it out first, Doc," Stillman said, motioning for Evans to stay back.

Stillman knocked on the door, keeping to the side in case the kid, in his delirium, squeezed off any rounds.

"Tommy, it's Sheriff Stillman. I'm here with Doc Evans. Can we come in?"

There was no reply. Stillman glanced at Evans, then at the corral where the cowboys watched him silently.

Stillman lifted the latch and the door squawked open on its rusty hinges. Peering into the musty shadows, he called, "Tommy?'

Evans stayed outside by the horses as Stillman disappeared into the bunkhouse. After a minute Stillman called to him. Clutching his black medical kit, Evans stepped through the door and walked about halfway down the row of bunks. Stillman was standing in the aisle, looking down.

Evans followed the sheriff's gaze to the kid lying on a lower bunk. Falk lay on his side, knees drawn nearly all the way to his chest, clutching a blood-soaked pillow to his head. He was breathing heavily and grunting and gritting his teeth. The knuckles clutching the pillow were bone-white.

On the floor beside the kid was a whiskey bottle and a silver-plated, scroll-engraved .45. Stillman picked up the gun and the bottle. He unloaded the gun, tossed it onto a distant bunk, and looked at the bottle. It was nearly empty. Glancing at Evans, he shrugged and set the bottle on the small table near the kid's head.

"The doc's here now, Tommy," Stillman said. "I'll leave you two alone here in a minute, but I'd just like to ask you one question."

The kid was wheezing and clutching the pillow. "I... I just wanna be left... alone...."

"I understand that, Tommy, but—"

"An' I'm gonna... I'm gonna *kill* that son of a devil!"

"I can understand your sentiment there, too, Tommy, but you're not going to have to. My deputy and I are going to hunt him down and bring him to justice. But I need to know why he attacked you boys last night."

" 'Cause he's crazy, that's why!" the kid shrieked, for the first time opening his eyes and glaring at Stillman.

"No other reason?" Stillman said. "He just broke into your cabin, killed the two others, and scalped you—for no reason whatsoever?"

"Just plumb loco's what he is ... damn that devil to hell! Look what he done to me!" The kid brought his knees to his chest tightly, convulsing with pain. "Ohhh! *God*, it hurts!"

"Easy, there, son," Evans said. "I've got something that's gonna make you feel better."

The kid swallowed and sucked a sharp breath. "The

only thing ... only thing that's gonna make me feel better is putting a bullet through that madman's brisket!"

Stillman glanced at the doctor. Evans returned the doubtful look.

"Well, I'll leave you two alone," Stillman said to the kid. To Evans he said, "Leon and I'll go up and check the cabin and try to cut Shambeau's trail from there. You'll probably head back to town later."

"Probably," Evans said, keeping his voice low. "There's really not much I can do except clean the wound and give the kid laudanum for his pain. It's just gonna take some time to scab up and heal. Won't even bandage it. It needs air."

"When you get back to town, will you stop by the school and tell Fay what's going on, let her know I'm tracking Shambeau? No telling how long it'll take."

Evans nodded. "Be careful, Ben. The man who did this has to be insane."

"Or madder than hell... about something," Stillman said.

He walked over to the blacksmith shop and found Leon standing before two open coffins propped on sawhorses. The deputy's arms were crossed on his chest as he pondered the bodies critically.

"What's it look like?" Stillman said.

"One was shot in the chest, right through the heart. The other had his throat cut."

Stillman walked over to the coffins and peered into each. He pursed his lips and shook his head.

"What'd the kid say?" Leon asked.

Stillman sighed. "Said he has no idea why Shambeau attacked them." He shook his head. "It just doesn't add up. I've seen ole Louis in town on several occasions, even talked to him some. He was odd, the way most loners are odd. Didn't have a whole lot to say. But he didn't seem crazy. Didn't seem *violent.*"

Leon nodded. "I traded with him some back when I had that roadhouse down by the Misery. He was a quiet fella. Like you said, maybe a little odd the way all those old mountain men are odd, but he didn't seem crazy. I couldn't see him doing somethin' like this unless ..."

Stillman looked at his deputy staring into the coffins. "Unless he was provoked?"

Leon raised his brows and nodded.

"Well," Stillman said after a while, "I guess it's time to go and have a little chat with Louis himself."

The two men turned from the coffins and headed for their horses. They were untying their reins from the hitch-rack when the cowboys filed toward them from the corral.

"Listen, Sheriff," one of them said. "Me and the boys been talkin' it over. Why don't you let us track this half-breed for you?"

Stillman glanced at Leon, then returned his eyes to the cowboy. "I appreciate the offer," he said with a friendly smile, "but it's my job. I'll do it."

He started to poke his boot through a stirrup but stopped when another man said, "You don't want to have to stay out in these mountains, trackin' that maniac. Why don't you deputize us; let us do it? You can go on home, where it's nice and warm, and we'll bring ole Louis back to Clantick to stand trial."

A smile pulled at the corners of his chapped mouth, and his slitted green eyes sparked a grin. "Unless of course he resists arrest. Then I reckon all bets are off."

The others smiled and snickered, shifting their feet, hooking their thumbs in their cartridge belts or fingering the butts of the hoglegs on their hips.

"You boys sure are generous," Leon quipped.

"And I appreciate it," Stillman said. "But like I said, no thanks."

"Aw, come on, Sheriff," the first man argued. "He killed two of our friends and scalped the kid. Now, the kid I never really cared for, but he's a Bar Seven man just the same, and we stand together. When that looney trapper attacked those boys, he as good as attacked us all. Now I say we have a right to settle this ourselves."

Stillman shook his head and was about to say something when another man cut in. "What the hell do you care, Stillman, if we do your job for you... nice and quiet-like? We'll hunt the man down, give him the necktie party he deserves, and keep our mouths shut. No one will know."

"But justice will sure as hell be served!" whooped a man from back of the group.

The others answered with whoops of their own.

"All right, quiet down!" Stillman shouted.

He waited for quiet. The Bar 7 men eyed him angrily.

"Now, my deputy and I are going to handle this. I appreciate your sentiment, but the fact of the matter is none of us really knows what happened out there last night. I intend to find out. This is a matter for the law, and since I'm the law, it's in my hands."

He lifted his arm and swept an angry finger across the crowd. "And if I see any of you out there, I'm going to haul you back to the hoosegow for interfering with lawmen in the performance of their duties. Do I make myself clear?"

No one said anything.

Stillman waited.

A square-jawed man with gray sideburns stared at him disdainfully, then wrinkled his mouth in a sneer. He spat, turned, and headed back toward the corral. The others followed him, sneering over their shoulders at the lawmen.

When he and Stillman had mounted their horses, Leon said, "I'd say you got through to them real good."

Stillman gave a rueful snort and gigged his horse back across the creek. He reined the bay to a halt before the house. Hendricks and his foreman, Dave Groom, were standing on the gallery drinking coffee.

"Hendricks," Stillman called. "Where's this woodcutting shack?"

When Hendricks had told him, Stillman said, "Make sure your men stay home, will you? If they interfere with me, I'm going to hold you personally responsible."

Then the sheriff and McMannigle gigged their horses southeastward along the creek.

Behind them, Hendricks cut his eyes at his foreman dubiously.

CHAPTER SIX

IT WAS AN EARLY noon when Stillman halted his horse on the two-track wagon trail rising through scattered aspens. He pointed at the cabin resting on a bench about a hundred yards above him and Leon, nestled among lodgepole pines.

The sun was bright, the sky clear and huge, the air crisp and sweet with the smell of pine resin. Steam lifted from the horses' backs; it had been a long, uphill climb.

"That must be it."

"Sure enough." Leon nodded.

His breath puffing in the air, Stillman gigged his horse ahead. Leon followed, his hand resting on his gun butt. It was doubtful the killer would have returned to the scene of the crime, but the fact that a murder had been committed here made both men edgy.

They rode around to the front of the cabin and dismounted. When he'd tied his horse to the hitching post, Stillman followed McMannigle inside where only two small windows offered light. Both men stood inside the door, looking silently around at the three pools of blood on the floor.

Finally, Stillman turned and inspected the door hanging

in the frame by only half of one leather hinge. The wood around the edge was splintered, as was the frame.

"Kicked in."

"He should've tried the latch," Leon said wryly. "I don't think it was lockable."

"Wanted to scare hell out of 'em, I guess."

"I have a feelin' that's just what he did, too. Probably cut the throat of the man standing here by the door, shot the other one there across the table. Shot the kid here and scalped him."

"Why do you suppose he scalped the kid?"

Leon shrugged. "Well, he's half Injun."

"He didn't scalp the others."

"The others didn't have much to scalp."

"There's a point." Stillman was looking around the room, at the bloodstains and broken furniture, at the cobwebs before the dirty, sashed windows, thinking it all through.

Grisly violence had happened here, and he just couldn't believe it was all due to a man going crazy. There had to be a more concrete reason than that. There usually was.

Finally, he sighed and turned to Leon. "I'm gonna have a smoke."

He turned and stepped through the door. He walked over to the small corral next to an arbor and stood with his back against the poles.

As Leon kicked around through the trees, looking for tracks and anything the killer might have left behind, anything that might give them a clue as to why this had occurred, Stillman rolled a cigarette and smoked it, pondering the cabin, trying to imagine all that had happened last night.

Finally, Leon wandered up and accepted the tobacco and papers Stillman offered. As the deputy built a cigarette, he said, "Found what looks to be his trail. He rode in from the east. Tied his horse by a big lodgepole pine right over yonder, about fifty yards up the mountain, and walked to the cabin. When he finished his business, he walked back to his horse, mounted up, and headed back east."

Leon struck a match and touched it to the quirley. "The ground's still damp from snowmelt and probably freezes every night. He left a good, clear trail. We shouldn't have any trouble runnin' him down."

Stillman nodded, staring absently at the cabin. After a while, he looked at his deputy. "Tell me what you know about him—Shambeau."

McMannigle took a long drag and blew it out slowly. "I heard he was born in Canada. His old man was a French trapper—a voyageur. His ma was Cree. When they both died, he lit out on his own and he's been alone ever since.

"At least, this is what I heard from other trappers and hiders. He used to stop by my roadhouse and trade hides for whiskey. Friendly enough, but he wasn't a talker. Always smelled like skunk. Must've used skunk oil in his lanterns back home, wherever home was. He never said and I never asked. I assumed it was probably down in the breaks somewhere. Probably has two or three cabins along his traplines."

Leon chuckled and flicked ashes from his cigarette. "A few times he offered me hides for an hour with my girl, Mary Beth, in my back room."

Leon chuckled, sucking in another long drag, and shook his head. "I told him I didn't do things that way, and he looked at me like I was daffy. How could I not think I was getting a deal?" Leon laughed again, dropping his chin and shaking his head.

"Ever see him violent?"

"Never. Surly, but not violent. Used to sleep on my floor, disappear first thing in the morning. Never heard a peep out of him. Never stole anything, and he had plenty of opportunities. Others like him sure did—wood, hay, horses." Leon glanced at Stillman, his right eyebrow cocked. "But I have a feeling if he ever got mad, he could do some damage. He ain't no little guy."

"I reckon that's what happened last night."

"Someone put a burr under his blanket?"

"Let's find out."

Stillman dropped his quirley stub, rubbed it out with his heel, and headed for his horse.

***

It was getting late in the afternoon, and they were crossing a high saddle when McMannigle reined his gray gelding to a halt, sniffing the air.

"What is it?" Stillman said.

"Do you smell smoke?"

Stillman reined Sweets to a stop and took several deep breaths. "Yeah, I think I caught a whiff of something. Where's it coming from?"

Quickly they dismounted and led their horses back down the game trail they'd been following until they were no longer visible from the other side of the divide. Stillman grabbed his field glasses off his saddle and crawled to the brow of the mountain, feeling the damp chill of the ground penetrating his denims and union suit.

They were a couple thousand feet high, and a fresh dusting of snow lay in the short, tawny grass and on the low-growing junipers. The sun was sinking, stretching shadows across the surrounding snub-nosed peaks, and the brittle breeze smelled tinny.

Adjusting the glasses, Stillman swept the small bowl beneath them from left to right. Bringing it back left, he lingered over an aspen copse. A thin shadow of what looked like smoke rose from the trees.

"I think we have our man," Stillman said. "Of course, it could be some line rider or another hunter."

"What is it?"

Stillman handed the glasses to McMannigle, who'd crawled up beside him. "Have a look at those aspens down there."

McMannigle took a long, careful look. "Yep, that's smoke all right. A cook fire, no doubt."

"Kind of careless, wouldn't you say?"

"No more careless than the trail he left—if it's him."

"Well, there's only one way to find out"

"How do you want to do it?"

Stillman drew his revolver and filled the empty chamber beneath the hammer, then spun the cylinder. Glancing down the saddle, he said, "Why don't you follow this ridgeline into those pines over there, come in from the south? I'll head over to the left and follow those shrubs into the aspens. Looks like some boulders and other good cover that way."

"All right. I'm going to get my rifle."

'Take these back to my horse, then, will you?" Stillman said, handing the glasses to Leon.

"You got it," the deputy said, turning away.

"Leon?"

"What's that?"

'Let's try to take him without shooting. We only know half the story so far."

"I hear that," McMannigle said, and headed down the hill to the horses idly cropping grass.

Stillman took another peek over the ridge, then stood and followed the brow of the saddle eastward, keeping low so the sky wouldn't outline him. When he saw that he was screened from the aspens, he crossed the ridge and headed down the other side, crouching behind boulders and shrubs.

At the base of the hill, he stopped behind a cedar, taking a reckoning and waiting for Leon to get into position on the other side of the aspens. He figured the deputy would need at least ten minutes.

Finally, he moved through a clump of junipers and ce-dars, staying low, his revolver held out before him. When he made the aspens, he slowed even more, watching his feet and avoiding branches, and crept from one tree to another.

The smoke from the cook fire got heavier. It smelled like aspen and roasting meat

When he'd walked about twenty yards into the copse, he came to a slight clearing fronted by a deadfall log. On the other side of the log, a column of smoke rose.

Stillman crept closer, extending the Colt, bringing more of the bivouac into view. There was a ring of stones at the fire's base. An aspen spit arced over the coals. Skewered on the spit, a small rabbit cooked, the juice dribbling into the coals and sizzling.

On another deadfall right of the fire, a riding saddle with a throw rope and a pack saddle had been draped. A rusty coffeepot sat on the log as well, its top lifted. Below it sat an uncorked, hide-covered canteen.

Suddenly several birds flew out of the aspens behind Stillman, crying shrilly. Instinctively he dived to his left and rolled as two quick shots resounded, the bullets cutting the air where he'd been crouching.

Lifting his .44 and seeing a shadow bound through the trees, he squeezed off four shots so quickly they sounded like one. A man yelled. The yell was followed by the sound of something big hitting the ground.

Stillman scrambled to his feet and ran toward the form lying over a branch. He stopped a few feet away and moved in slowly, his eyes riveted on the prone figure.

It was Shambeau, all right, in hide breeches and a buffalo coat. He was a large, bearded man with long salt-and-pepper hair parted in the middle. His nose was broad, eyes sunk deep in his rawboned, deep-lined face. A ragged white scar crept from the bridge of his nose to his left temple.

Blood shone wetly on his chest, just below his shoulder. Not far away, an old Colt Navy with a brass trigger guard lay in the leaves.

Hearing the distant footfalls of McMannigle running toward him from the other side of the camp, Stillman stepped forward cautiously. He watched the trapper's inert face, the closed eyes not even twitching.

Sliding his gaze to the Colt Navy, Stillman took a step toward it, intending to kick it away, when his ears shuddered with a sudden cry. Out of the corner of his eye, he saw a flash of movement

Shambeau was rising, bounding toward him. Before Stillman could fire, the man was on him, and the gun was flying out of his hand.

The trapper bulled into Stillman from a crouched position, lifting him off his feet and throwing him over backward. Stillman hit the ground hard, the back of his head taking the brunt of the fall. It stunned him for a moment, his vision dancing.

When he saw the trapper reaching for a knife on his belt, Stillman lifted his right leg and kneed the man sideways, then swung his left fist, connecting soundly with the man's stony jaw. As Shambeau flew off of him, Stillman bolted to his feet and glanced around for his gun. Not seeing it, he returned his eyes to the trapper—too late. The man scissor-kicked

Stillman's feet out from under him, and the ground came up hard against the sheriff's side, grieving both shoulders and collarbone.

In spite of the pain, he regained his legs quickly as Shambeau, snarling like a savage, dark eyes wide and shiny, bulled into him again, thrusting him into a tree, making his head pound and his ears ring.

The trapper pulled his arm back and brought his fist forward, sinking it deep in Stillman's gut. Trying to suck air back into his lungs, Stillman lowered his head and whipped it up quickly into Shambeau's jaw.

The man staggered backward. Stillman followed, swinging, connecting a roundhouse right with the man's cheekbone. Shambeau straightened and swung his own right. Stillman ducked under it, but when he came up, Shambeau gave him a hard left jab.

Dazed, vaguely amazed at the enormous strength behind the man's fists, Stillman floundered backward. Before he could recover, the trapper jabbed him again in the jaw, whipping Stillman's head back. Another hard right to the forehead buckled one of his knees, which sank to the ground.

When Stillman lifted his eyes, Shambeau was moving in for the kill, wielding not only a savage grin but a big, broad-bladed bowie with an edge sharp enough to cut a stout rope with a single slash. Shambeau whipped the knife sideways, cocking the arm to bring the blade forward across Stillman's neck.

It was a stillborn movement, ending just as the blade started forward. Stillman saw something move behind the trapper, whose head jerked forward, his chin bouncing off his chest.

The man stiffened and his eyes seemed to focus on something in the far distance behind Stillman. Then they rolled up and his face slackened, as if all the muscles had been cut, and the man sank to his knees. He fell forward with a resolute groan and lay still, his face in the grass.

"What in the hell took you so long?" Stillman said, staring up at the face of Leon McMannigle, who was still holding the rifle he'd used on Shambeau, butt forward.

"I tried to get here as fast as I could, Sheriff." Leon's sober face suddenly opened with a toothy grin. "How you feelin'?"

CHAPTER SEVEN

WHILE STILLMAN RUBBED his jaw and tried to recover his senses, McMannigle cuffed Shambeau's hands behind his back and tied his ankles loosely with rawhide. The trapper moaned and spat as he came out of it, turning his head from side to side.

Stillman climbed heavily to his feet, found his Stetson, dusted it off, and donned it. Then he reloaded his Colt and dropped it back in his holster. He stood looking down at the broad-backed trapper, who growled and spat like an animal caught in a snare.

Stillman turned to Leon, who was watching the trapper warily. "Why don't you get the horses? We'll camp here tonight, get an early start in the morning."

"He ain't happy," Leon said, watching the shaggy-headed Shambeau try to wrestle his wrists from the cuffs.

"No, but maybe I can hold him"—Stillman sighed, his expression wry—"now that you've brained and hogtied him."

Leon looked at Stillman and winced. "Your face looks like hamburger."

"You should see my pride."

Leon wagged his head and started walking toward the ridge, branches snapping under his feet.

Stillman squatted on his haunches beside the trapper. "No use fighting it, Louis. Those cuffs aren't going anywhere. Neither's the rawhide. You try to run, you won't get far."

Shambeau flopped onto his back and raged, *"Let me go! Damn you to hell!"*

Stillman shook his head. "You're not going anywhere. I'm Ben Stillman, sheriff of Hill County. I'm arresting you for the murder of two Bar 7 men and the assault on one more."

The man's features relaxed a little, and his eyes found the badge on Stillman's buckskin mackinaw. For the first time, the eyes lost their animal rage and cunning, and an intelligent light glowed dully, far back in their flinty hardness.

"They shot my mule."

His voice was flat and owned a peculiar accent—the nasality of French mixed with the hard, flat consonants of Indian.

"What's that?"

"The kid shot my mule." He pronounced *kid* "kit."

Stillman frowned. "Where? When?"

Shambeau was half sitting on his butt, head lifted off the ground, the cords in his neck straining as if to pull through his hide. "Yesterday. I passed them on my way to the creek"—he jutted his chin to indicate north—"to check my traps. They were cutting the wood. The kid shot my mule." He tensed suddenly, giving a look of intense pain and glanced down at his shoulder where the bloodstain was growing, matting the curly, cinnamon fur of his coat.

"The bullet go all the way through or is it still in there?" Stillman asked.

"She still in," Shambeau said with a sour look on his face.

"As soon as my deputy returns with the horses, I'll put a compress on it. We'll get you to a doctor tomorrow."

"I don't want a doctor. I got traplines to tend."

"That'll be a while, I'm afraid. That kid might've shot your mule, but you had no right to go on a rampage."

Shambeau looked at him, and the animal rage returned to his gaze. "They shot my mule! I had to build a cache in trees! To my cabin it is a three-day ride!"

Stillman scowled. "Sorry," he said. "I know how you feel, but that ain't enough to call what you did justifiable homicide. Not anymore, it isn't."

"To call... it is *what?*"

"Never mind. If you get to your feet, I'll help you back to your fire."

"Turn me loose, lawman!"

"Can't do that, Shambeau. You committed both murder and assault." Stillman stood. "Now get up, and I'll help you back to the fire. Any funny business, I'll leave you here to bleed to death."

Stillman helped the man back to the bivouac and eased him down beside the fire. He removed the charred rabbit from the spit and tossed it into the trees. Then he threw more wood on the fire and sat down on one of the dead-falls to wait for McMannigle and the horses.

Sitting there, he leaned forward, set his elbows on his knees, and laced his hands together, watching the trapper. Shambeau sat with his back against the other deadfall, legs spread before him, breathing heavily, a perpetual snarl on his lips, his hair in his face.

The picture of defeat.

Stillman couldn't help feeling sorry for the man. Sorrier than he'd felt for the men he'd killed and the kid he'd scalped. The Bar 7 men had started the whole thing when the kid had shot the mule. Stillman suspected the two older gents had done little to discourage him before or to reprimand him after.

Shambeau was an inscrutable loner, a maverick mountain man, and a Métis to boot. Any one of those things would have made him a black sheep, but all three together made him a renegade—a man to be feared and shunned. A man to treat as you would a wolf preying on your livestock, a coyote making the calving rounds.

So, they'd shot his mule for a joke or out of spite for the man and his outdated ways. Why else would they have done it?

Shambeau was just getting even the only way he knew. True, he'd done more than get even for a dead mule, but he was a frontiersman, and the only justice he knew was the frontier kind. Stillman, a frontiersman himself, knew that frontier justice was almost always swift and never pretty.

He did not personally hold the action against the trapper, but since the law held it against the man, and since Stillman represented the law, he had to hold it against him professionally. He had to take him in and haul him before a judge.

It occurred to him now, with a poignant sense of loss, that Fay had been right: This wasn't really the frontier anymore. While true frontiersmen still wandered here and there about the West, the West wasn't what it used to be. The railroad had come and the buffalo had gone and most of the Indians were subsisting on reservations. And men like Stillman, who'd grown up on the frontier and had changed with the times, had to haul men like Louis Shambeau, who had not, before a court of civilized law to answer for their crimes against civilization.

It was a hell of an ugly job, and Stillman had the undeniable urge to let the man go. But if he did that, he'd have to turn in his badge. While so-called "civilization" often made him feel like he'd chugged a quart of sour milk, he wasn't yet ready to throw in the towel. Especially not after he'd dragged Fay all the way out here from Denver.

No, there was no denying it, Stillman thought now, pondering the man who'd beaten him—he was a civilized man. And that meant that, like civilization, there was a lot about himself he didn't like.

Not the least of which, at the moment, was his job.

When McMannigle appeared with the horses, Stillman stood and retrieved a spare shirt from his saddlebags and tore it into strips.

"Sit still now, Shambeau. I'm going to apply a compress to that bullet wound."

The trapper said nothing, just stared into the flames, the sneer still curling his mouth.

When Stillman hunkered down on his haunches to slide the tunic off the man's shoulder, he could smell the skunky, gamey odor of his clothes, saw the translucent specs of lice in his hair down close to his scalp. It had been a long time since Stillman had been around a man who smelled this bad—probably not since his old hide-hunting days with his friend, Bill Harmon—and he couldn't help wrinkling his nose as he tended the man's shoulder. Aside from the smell of skunk, he smelled like a roast that had cured too long in the sun.

There were some things he didn't mind about civilization, thought the sheriff. Namely, baths.

When he'd finished the chore, he stood with what remained of his shirt and saw that Leon was stringing a picket line for the horses, both of which he'd unsaddled and rubbed down with grass. The trapper's spotted pony stood ground-staked nearby, nervous in the presence of strangers.

"Got any whiskey?" Stillman called to him. Stillman himself had given up hard liquor after a long bout with the bottle after that soiled dove had shot him in the back and he'd had to retire his Deputy U.S. Marshal's badge.

"In my saddlebags," Leon said.

Stillman fished the bottle and a tin cup out of the deputy's gear, poured a shot for Shambeau, and brought it to him. "Here you go," he said. "That should help with the pain."

"I don't want any of your stinking liquor," Shambeau spat, not looking at him.

"Have it your way," Stillman said.

He set the cup on a rock by the fire, knowing McMannigle would no doubt want it after his chores. Then he went to his own gear and fished out a pot and a bag of beans. As he prepared a meager supper of beans and coffee, he stole several glances at the trapper, who sat in the fading light, gazing sullenly into the fire.

As the dark closed in, the dancing fire found the hard, weather-scaled plains of the trapper's face. It shone in the dark eyes, which seemed to absorb everything, giving back nothing.

Stillman and McMannigle turned in early, rolling up in their soogans just after full dark. Stillman had lain several blankets beside the trapper, but the man ignored them, choosing instead to sit where Stillman had deposited him earlier, staring into the fire, brooding.

"Gives me the creeps," Leon said, glancing at the prisoner as he squirmed around in his blankets, getting comfortable.

"You tied him good and tight to the log, didn't you?"

Leon nodded. "He still gives me the creeps." He sighed, yawned, smacked his lips, and closed his eyes.

"Yeah ... me, too," Stillman said, tipping his Stetson over his face.

He woke up several times during the long, cold night and tossed wood on the fire. A few times he saw the trapper sleeping with his chin on his chest, but mostly he appeared awake and staring into the darkness beyond the fire's guttering glow.

What was he thinking about, anyway? Probably escape, Stillman figured, and made a mental note to keep an extra eye on the man tomorrow. Wounded or not, he had the strength of a grizzly bear and would no doubt try to escape at the first opportunity, no matter how slim his chance of success.

The next morning Stillman and McMannigle rose at first light. After a hurried breakfast of pan bread and coffee, which the trapper refused, the three men mounted their horses and headed north toward Clantick.

Stillman rode point, the trapper following on his spotted cayuse, his reins in Stillman's hand, his wrists tethered behind his back, his ankles bound to his stirrups. Leon rode behind the man, his rifle in his arms, his eyes skinned on the dangerous, brooding figure before him.

They stopped at noon for a half-hour lunch and to rest their horses. About four o'clock Clantick appeared on the horizon, smoke lifting from the shanties at the edge of town. Stillman sighed with relief. It had been a long ride. He was eager to have this ugly business finished, and to see Fay again.

When they hit town, several stray dogs ran out to nip at their horses' hocks. They took French Street past Stillman's white frame house to First Street, and hung a left westward toward Doc Evans's place, where they'd wait while Evans tended the trapper's shoulder.

As they rode down First, people halted on the boardwalks

to stare at the two lawmen and their prisoner. The trapper rode crouched in his saddle, favoring his wounded shoulder. His long, greasy hair hid his face. He hadn't said a word the entire trip.

Evelyn Vincent, the waitress at Sam Wa's, stepped outside the cafe on Stillman's left and waved. Stillman tipped his hat to her. He was turning his gaze back westward when he saw several men pour out of the Drovers Saloon and step into the street before him.

There were over a half dozen men, he saw now, all dressed in battered drovers hats and chaps. All but the man in the lead, that was. He appeared younger and thinner than the others, and he wore a red bandanna over the top of his head and knotted at the base of his skull.

Sticking out around the bandanna were chestnut locks of full, rich hair.

"Oh, crap," Stillman heard Leon mutter behind him.

Oh crap, was right.

"Tommy," Stillman said, bringing his horse to a halt, trying to keep his voice even, "did you shoot this man's mule?"

The kid shrugged. "So what if I did? It was just a mule. Ain't no excuse for what he did to us."

Stillman pondered the lad grimly, then nodded. "Well, we got him. Justice is served. Out of the way."

The kid had stopped in the street directly before Stillman, his face expressionless, his long hair ruffling in the cool spring breeze, his hand draped over the silver-plated pistol resting in his hand-tooled black holster. The other men had stopped in the street to the kid's right, their squinting, insolent eyes on the trapper, their thumbs hooked behind their cartridge belts. The breeze toyed with their chaps and their hat brims, fluttered the colored bandannas tied around their necks.

"Justice is served, is it?" the kid snarled. "I ain't got any hair on the top of my head."

One of the cowboys let loose a chuckle deep in his throat, but quickly stifled it. The kid turned to the man with a savage scowl.

Leon cleared his throat. "You know, I heard toupee makers are doin' just wonderful things with horsehair these days."

Stillman turned in his saddle and gave the deputy a scowl.

Leon shrugged. "Just tryin' to help."

"I'll tell you how justice is gonna be served," the kid sneered, drawing his revolver and turning to the trapper slouched in his saddle.

Stillman lifted his right leg over the saddle horn and slid down from his horse. He grabbed the kid's gun with his left hand and punched the side of the kid's head with his right. Releasing the gun, the kid went down on a knee, yelling, "Ow! Damn you—!"

The kid stood, staggering, and drew the knife from his belt sheath, wielding it menacingly at the sheriff. Stillman kicked the knife out of the kid's hand, stepped in, and slammed another right in the kid's face. The kid fell hard, screaming. Stillman crouched, grabbed the kid's collar, and held him with his left hand while he let him have it, over and over, with his right.

He lost all sense of himself, giving into a red-hot anger burning up from deep within. As if from far away he could hear the cowboys yelling their objections. From even farther off, he heard Leon.

"Ben! Ben! Damnit! *Ben!*"

Finally, the voice became distinct, and Stillman, realizing suddenly what he was doing, froze, his fist drawn back. He glanced over at Leon, still sitting his steel-dust, a flush glowing behind the mahogany of his clean-lined face, his inky eyes urgent, pleading, his eyebrows furrowed.

"Ben, you'll kill him!"

Breathing hard, jaws tight, Stillman looked at the kid who hung nearly unconscious in the grip of his left fist. Red bruises were blossoming on his cheeks and blood dripped from his smashed mouth. His bandanna had slid halfway off his head, and Stillman could see the raw red swath where his hair used to be.

Lifting his gaze, Stillman saw the cowboys gathered about him, crouched and exasperated, hands on their guns but knowing if they drew, the deputy would no doubt plug them with the Spencer carbine in his arms.

Sighing, Stillman released the kid, who fell on his back, groaning. Stillman looked around for the kid's gun and his knife. Seeing them in the dust, he picked them up and stuffed the knife under his cartridge belt. He held the gun up, opened the cylinder, and shook the six cartridges out.

When he'd wedged the gun behind his belt, Stillman

said to the kid who still lay on his back, moaning and groaning and trying to regain his faculties, "You can pick up your weapons at my office in a month."

Lifting his gaze to the others he said, "If I see any of you in town within the next two weeks, I'm turning the key on you. Understand?"

"But, Sheriff," one of the drovers objected, "that crazy polecat *scalped* the kid and *killed* two of our friends!"

"That's why he's in my custody. Now do as I told you, or I'll throw you in the hoosegow pronto!"

Stillman's anger was back in earnest. He had no time for these rabble-rousers. It was the kid and the two other Bar 7 men who had instigated this mess, and now Stillman was having to clean up after them, arresting a man for seeking the only justice he knew. A man who lived alone and bothered no one unless they bothered him. A man who now would no doubt hang because one snot-nosed kid and two cow-brained drovers shot his mule.

"Take the kid and get the hell out of town!" Stillman raged, waving an arm.

The cowboys gave a start, backing off. Then two of them went over to the kid and helped him to his feet. When they were all heading down the boardwalk toward the livery barn, the kid jerking angry looks behind him, Stillman sighed, removed his hand from his holstered Colt, and swung up into the saddle.

Glancing around, he saw that more people had lined the boardwalks, observing the spectacle. Even the Chinaman, Sam Wa, stood there beside his waitress, Evelyn Vincent.

Guiltily averting his eyes, embarrassed that he'd lost his temper in so public a place, Stillman mumbled, "Let's go," and spurred his horse westward toward Evans's place at the top of the hill.

CHAPTER EIGHT

A MATRONLY WOMAN and a young boy with his right arm in a sling were climbing into a wagon as Stillman, the trapper, and McMannigle topped the hill and pulled their horses up to the doctor's front gate. As the woman released the wagon's brake and took up her reins, she eyed the grizzled trapper with bald disdain, her pug nose wrinkled.

"Mornin', Mrs. Doherty," Stillman hailed the woman, tipping his hat.

She did not respond. Instead, she turned sharply from the trapper with a loud "Harumph!" and flicked the reins against her sorrel's back. As the buggy passed, the boy swung around in his seat, watching the trapper with wide-eyed fascination.

Stillman and McMannigle tied their horses to the hitching post and helped the trapper out of his saddle. The man kicked his moccasined feet free of the stirrups and hit the ground with a snarl and a loud sigh. The wound had opened, and the bandage was bloody. He was in obvious pain, throwing his head back and stretching his dry lips away from his big, chipped teeth.

Stillman on one side, McMannigle on the other, they guided the trapper through the gate and toward the house. The doctor was standing in the open door.

"I sure wish you'd try to bring your prisoners in without shooting them, Sheriff," he said. "Few have ever had any money to pay for my services."

"I'll see to it the town council reimburses you," Stillman replied as he and Leon led the man through the door.

"They'll just send over some hay," the doctor carped, closing the door behind them. "Believe me, I have plenty of hay."

Katherine Kemmett was coming out of the examining room with a load of medical tools to be cleaned. "Oh, dear," she said, seeing the big, hairy man Stillman and Mc-Mannigle were ushering through the foyer.

"In there," Evans said, meaning the room Katherine had just vacated. "Have him take a seat on the gurney. Good Lord, what's that smell?"

"Your patient," Leon said.

When they had him in the room, Stillman backed Shambeau up to the examining table. The trapper resisted, obviously disgruntled with his unfamiliar surroundings. Stillman wondered if the man had ever been in a real house before.

"It's all right, Louis," Leon said. "The doctor's gonna dig that bullet out of your hide."

Shambeau jerked a hard look at the deputy. "So you can hang me? Why not shoot me now... get it over with?"

"We don't know you're gonna hang," Stillman said,

trying to sound reassuring. "I'll make sure the judge knows the whole story. When he finds out they shot your mule, he might go easy on you."

The prisoner cursed in French. At least it sounded like French to Stillman.

"Just the same, sit down there, nice and easy. The doc's gonna look you over."

Reluctantly the big man sat on the table, twisting his neck and rolling his head with the pain of the bullet in his shoulder. The doctor and Mrs. Kemmett came in, Katherine wiping her wet hands on a clean, white towel.

"All right, boys," Evans said. "You can step outside while I have a look at him."

Stillman shook his head. "We have to stay and make sure he doesn't try and run for it."

"In his condition, he wouldn't get far." Evans tugged the buffalo coat off the trapper's raw, bloody shoulder, which had turned a mottled purple. "Besides that, you might as well bank on him being here overnight. I can already tell I'll have to do some deep cutting to get that bullet out, which means I'll be putting him under with ether. He'll be out till morning, at least."

Leon turned to Stillman as the doctor examined the trapper's shoulder. "Why don't you head on home, Ben? I'll stay here with Shambeau."

Stillman thought it over and nodded. "All right I'll get a meal in me and take a nap. I'll be back over to relieve you later this evening."

Evans glanced at him. "I should have a look at that face of yours, Ben."

"You got your hands full, Doc. I'll have Fay clean it up."

"Stay home with that pretty wife of yours," Leon told Stillman. "I can nap here while the doc has ole Louis under the knife. I bet Mrs. Kemmett would rustle me up some grub if I begged her hard enough."

Katherine glanced away from observing the doctor's work to flash Leon a smile. "I might be able to rustle you up something from Clyde's icebox."

"All right, then," Stillman said. "I'll head over in the morning. Maybe by then we can move him over to the jail. In the meantime, I'll telegraph a message to the circuit judge, see if we can't get him here pronto."

He gave his deputy's shoulder a friendly squeeze and headed outside to his horse. After mounting up, he headed back down the hill, leading Shambeau's spotted Indian pony.

His first order of business was to get rid of the trapper's horse, which he did at Auld's Livery Barn, having Auld stable the animal and store the trapper's gear until after the trial. That task accomplished, Stillman headed over to the telegraph office, where he scribbled out a message for the agent to send to Judge Herman Watkins.

Finding no messages on the door of the jailhouse, he led Sweets out to the back stable. When he'd unsaddled the tired horse, he grained, watered, and curried him, and let him into the small pole corral where the bay promptly got down and rolled luxuriously in the well-churned dust.

It was well past five by the time Stillman was walking

east on First Street, where shadows were falling away from the tall facades and the traffic was dwindling. Taking a chance that Fay was still at school grading papers and cleaning chalkboards, Stillman went on past French Street, where his and Fay's house lay, and headed for the white-frame school, which sat in a little hollow at the eastern edge of town.

Stillman was right. His lovely schoolteacher was hard at work scrubbing off the students' desktops as he knocked and entered through the front door.

"Ben!" She dropped her rag in the wooden bucket and ran to him, throwing her arms around his neck. "Oh, I'm so glad you're back! I was worried I'd have to go home to an empty house again tonight."

"No, we got him," Stillman said, trying to sound perky.

She pulled away from him to look him over. Her brows furrowed and her cheeks flushed as she scrutinized his battered face. "Oh, Ben!"

"Yeah, I got a little careless, but I'm fine."

"You're fine? Your cheeks are purple, there's a gash on your brow and another, bigger one on your lip!"

"The man packs a hell of a punch," he said with a sigh, "but I'm alright. Really." He returned Fay's appraising look, saw her hair falling over her shoulders and around the full breasts swelling her crisp schoolteacher's dress, and, in spite of his bruised and battered body, knew a moment of sweet desire.

"How much more do you have to do here?"

"Just blow out the lamps. I was lingering because I didn't know you were back."

"Come on, then," he said, squeezing her shoulders eagerly. "Let's go get a steak over at Sam Wa's, then head home for a little promenade."

Fay laughed huskily and took his face gently in her soft hands. "You are all right, aren't you?" She kissed him tenderly.

"Never better."

When she'd blown out the lamps and closed the damper on the woodstove, she grabbed her shawl and stepped through the door Stillman was holding open.

As they turned through the schoolyard gate and headed westward up First Street, Stillman nodding to a prominent rancher and his wife heading out of town on their red-wheeled surrey, Fay asked him about Shambeau. Stillman told her what had happened, and that Doc Evans was sewing him up. He left out the part about his using Tommy Falk's face as a punching bag on First Street a while ago.

"They shot his mule?"

"That's what it looks like. The kid will get called to testify at the trial. It'll all come out then, if I have to beat it out of the little rodent myself."

"Why would they do such a thing?"

"For sport," Stillman said. "And because they didn't know any better than to harass a man who wanted only to be left alone."

Fay looked at him. "Sounds like you're on his side."

Stillman took Fay's hand as they mounted the boardwalk on the south side of the street. "I know I'm not supposed to be on anyone's side, Fay, but damnit, the man was minding his own business!"

"He didn't have to do what he did. He could have come to you and reported it."

Stillman exhaled heavily and shook his head. "That's just not the way of men like Shambeau. They were out here long before there were any laws besides the ones they enforced themselves, in their own way."

"Times change."

Stillman sighed again regretfully as he opened the door of Sam Wa's Cafe. "Yes, they do."

The cafe was almost empty but for a couple retired farmers sipping coffee at the counter. As Fay made her way to a table, Stillman asked the waitress, Evelyn Vincent, if he could wash before he ate, then headed into the kitchen where a basin sat on a food preparation table.

The cafe's proprietor, the venerable Sam Wa, stood at the range stirring a big pot of chili. Seeing Stillman, he bowed and said, "Good work today, Ben! Very good work! That Falk kid needed a good ass-kicking for long time!"

"Yeah, I lost my temper, though, Sam. Not very professional, I'm afraid."

"Ah, screw professional. This the wild and woolly West, no?" The stout Chinaman in a blue smock and stained apron threw his head back and laughed raucously as only Saw Wa could laugh.

"That's what I used to think, Sam."

Stillman dried his hands, arms, and face on a towel, dabbing gingerly at the cuts, and headed for the swinging doors.

"The missus with you?" Wa called to him.

"She sure is, Sam."

"What you have—steak?"

"Two T-bones, Sam. I'll have mine—"

"I know, I know—you have yours rare, the missus have hers well-done. Ha! Ha! Ha!"

Stillman smiled, waved, and headed back to the eating area where the young Evelyn Vincent was talking with Fay. As Stillman sat down, Evelyn turned to him.

"Fay told me what happened with Louis Shambeau," she said. "I could've told you that if Tommy Falk was involved, he was the one who instigated the trouble."

"Well, I don't know that for sure, Evelyn. We'll have to let a jury decide."

"Poor Louis," Evelyn said. "All he ever wanted was to be left alone. Never gave me a lick of trouble the few times he came in here. Tommy Falk's never been anything *but* trouble." She leaned close to Stillman. "*I* can't tell you how thrilled I was when I saw you thrashin' him in the street earlier." She snickered. "Now, what can I get you two?"

"Sam already has our orders," Stillman said. "Steak with all the trimmings."

"You got it," Evelyn said, scribbling on her notepad and wheeling for the kitchen.

When she was gone, Fay said, "Thrashing him in the street earlier'?"

Stillman hemmed and hawed, cleared his throat. Scratching his head, he said, "Well, the little pipsqueak went after Louis with a gun."

"That's awful," Fay said. "But are you sure you didn't use a little more force than necessary?"

"No, I'm not," Stillman admitted.

Fay studied him across the table. "This case really has your blood boiling, doesn't it?"

"Yes, I guess it does. I grew up with guys like Louis. Me and ole Bill Harmon used to hunt buffalo with 'em— back when there were still buffalo to hunt. I learned a lot from them, and I learned how they thought. A man kills your mule—it may seem harsh—but that man dies. It's a matter of principle. It lets others know you're not a man to be trifled with. Tough rules for a tough time and a tough land."

"But that time is gone, and that land is changing."

"Not in Louis's mind."

"Maybe not in yours, either, eh?"

Stillman shrugged.

Fay said, "Or maybe there's just a part of you that doesn't want to let it go. I can see the appeal. It was a simpler time." She smiled. "And you were young."

The steaks came and they ate, washing the meal down with hot coffee and following it up with apricot pie and ice cream. When they finished, Stillman paid the bill, and he and Fay walked home glancing over their shoulders to watch the sun set behind the buttes west of town.

"You go get out of those dirty clothes," Fay said as they walked into the house. "I'll get a fire going in the stove and heat some water for a bath."

"Mrs. Stillman, I do believe you're conniving to see me naked!"

"Well, it has been two days." Fay laughed, heading into the kitchen.

"What about my chickens?"

"I had one of the boys come over and feed them after school. Out of those clothes!"

Later, he soaked in the tub while Fay sponged his back. He was brooding, staring into a corner of the kitchen.

"Let it go, Ben," she said softly. "You did your job. Now you have to leave it up to the judge."

"I reckon you're right," he said. "It's just that... he's so ... out of his element." He looked at her. "You know, if I could I'd let him go."

Fay sighed. "I think it's time to retire to the other room, Mr. Stillman."

Stillman frowned. "I ain't tired."

"Neither am I, Mr. Stillman."

He turned to see her reaching behind to unbutton her dress and draw it down her shoulders. "Oh, these old schoolmarm dresses get so confining...."

"I imagine they do at that," he said, staring at the straining white cotton of her chemise.

"I bet I can help you with that scowl on your face, Mr. Stillman," she said, and he watched her hands slip into the sudsy water between his knees.

"Yes, ma'am... I bet you can at that."

As her hands moved in the water, Stillman unlaced her camisole and slid it down her arms. She inhaled sharply as he kissed her slender neck and nuzzled her breasts.

Later, after they'd made love in their room and she'd fallen asleep, Stillman got up and dressed in his union suit. He went out to the living room and stoked the stove, then built and lit a cigarette. He stood by the window, smoking, thinking about the trapper, thinking about the old days when he and the incorrigible Bill Harmon had been young and running wild across the West.

Odd to think of Bill dead now, buried beside his Indian wife in the Two-Bears. As gone as the buffalo...

Finally, Stillman's mind returned to the present, and he considered dressing and heading up to Evans's place on the hilltop to check on things. He decided against it. The trapper would be under the ether until morning, the doctor had said.

Everything would be fine.

Stillman stubbed out his cigarette and returned to the bedroom where Fay slept with her long legs curled beneath the quilts, her chocolate hair awash across her pillow. He crawled in beside her, kissed a tender breast, and nestled his face against her belly.

Everything would be fine, and he would feel young again soon.

CHAPTER NINE

LEON MCMANNIGLE WAS sound asleep on the fainting couch in Doc Evans's parlor when he heard a door open and Evans and his assistant, Mrs. Kemmett, conversing. Instantly awake, the deputy sat up and dropped his feet to the floor, blinking and shaking his head.

Straightening his gun belt, he headed for the kitchen where Doc Evans and Mrs. Kemmett were placing bloody surgical instruments in a porcelain pan.

"How'd it go, Doc?" Leon asked.

Evans removed his surgical mask. "Not too bad. The bullet had hit a bone but didn't break it. I think he'll be all right."

"He still out?"

Evans nodded. "Oh, he'll be out for quite some time. You don't have to worry about him. Sleepin' like a baby." Evans frowned and wrinkled his nose as he washed his hands and arms in a steaming kettle on the stove. "A rather smelly baby, however."

"Why, Clyde," Katherine Kemmett exclaimed in a mocking tone, "how sensitive your nose has become.

It certainly couldn't have been that sensitive before I started cleaning up after you." She glanced at McMannigle. "You should have seen the mess I found in here, Leon. Just scandalous!"

"Oh, Katherine, I don't think it was that bad."

"No, it was worse."

Leon chuckled and wagged his head. "I swear if I didn't know better, I'd say you two were married."

Right away he knew he'd said the wrong thing. Neither Evans nor Mrs. Kemmett said a word. She fooled with the instruments boiling on the stove, and Evans's cheeks shone vaguely red as he dried his hands on a clean towel.

"Well," the doctor said with a sigh, changing the subject and glancing at Leon, "I suppose you'll be here till your prisoner wakes up?"

"I can't let him out of my sight, no matter how deep asleep he is. Sorry. I hate to put you out, Doc... Mrs. Kemmett."

"Not at all," Katherine said. "I have to fix Clyde's supper as he's absolutely useless in the kitchen. I might as well fix yours while I'm at it. Then I have to get over to Mrs. Grenville's place."

"Oh, is she sick?" Leon asked.

"Yes, but not in a bad way," Katherine said, her prim cheeks coloring a little.

"She's about to deliver," Evans said, placing his open hand along his mouth, as though sharing a secret.

"Clyde!" Katherine scolded him.

"Oh, for God's sakes, Katherine. There's nothing scandalous about giving birth. My mother did it, Leon's mother did it, and, yes, even your pious mother did it— though how in the hell she ever got pregnant, I can't imagine!" Evans glanced at Leon and grinned devilishly.

"Such talk, Clyde. Another man comes around, and you lose all sense. Well, I'm not listening to another word!"

With that she produced two beefsteaks from the icebox and dropped them into a fry pan on the range.

Evans opened a cabinet over the icebox and produced a bottle. "A predinner libation, my good man?" he said to Leon as he dropped heavily into a chair at the small kitchen table.

Leon's mouth watered at the sight of the bottle in the doctor's hands, but he turned a wary eye to Mrs. Kemmett, the minister's widow.

"Oh, don't worry about me, Leon," Katherine said as she sliced potatoes into a pan. "I'm quite used to the doctor's 'libations,' as he calls them. They don't bother me a bit." She turned to Evans pouring several fingers of whiskey in two water glasses. "As long as he uses moderation and it doesn't interfere with our practice, that is."

Leon frowned, puzzled. " 'Our' practice?"

Evans shrugged and scowled down at his drink. "Yes ... well... she's become a ... partner. In the business," he was quick to add. "She's still my assistant but has combined her midwife practice with my medical practice. So, we're ... partners."

Katherine smiled, self-satisfied.

McMannigle cut his eyes between them and nodded slowly. "Well, I guess one drink wouldn't hurt," he said, eagerly taking a chair across from the doctor.

Evans shoved a glass over to Leon's side of the table and lifted his own in salute. "To all good things in moderation!" he said with a wink.

Leon shrugged his shoulders and cracked a smile that set his inky black eyes ablaze. Obviously, there was more of a flirtation going on here than either of these two realized. "To partners!" he said, nudging Evans's glass with his own.

The doctor only scowled at him suspiciously, saying nothing. Neither did Katherine. Grinning, Leon threw back half his whiskey and set his glass back down on the table.

Before Katherine left, Evans finished his drink and made a show of returning the bottle to a cabinet. As soon as she'd gone, having shoveled the steaks and fried potatoes onto two plates and setting the plates on the table. Evans retrieved the bottle with a devilish chuckle and tipped it over Leon's glass.

"Better not, Doc," the deputy said, waving him off. "I best stay clear this evenin'."

"Clear for what? Him?" Evans gestured at the closed door to the examining room. "I told you, he'll be out till morning. I doubt he'll even start batting his eyes before noon."

"You sure about that?"

"Certain-sure."

"Well, all right, then. I guess one more drink won't hurt."

Evans talked the thirsty, trail-sore deputy into one more

drink before they dug into their suppers, and, reassuring the man that the trapper was dead to the world, into "just one more" when their plates were cleaned.

"Well, you up to some poker?" Evans asked as he dropped their plates into a pan of water simmering on the stove.

McMannigle had checked on the sleeping trapper and was softly closing the examining room door. "Ah, you don't have to entertain me, Doc. Go on about your business."

"Where's my business?" Evans said, looking around. "The only patient I have is in there dead to the world. Normally, I'd head down to the Drovers to skin the cow-pokes at five-card-stud, but I reckon I'd better keep an eye on ole Shambeau. So, it's just you and me. Why not entertain each other over a friendly game of cards?"

Leon cocked his head suspiciously and frowned. "Okay, but you aren't gonna try to get me to drink with you, too, are you?"

Evans held up the bottle. "You aren't gonna make me drink alone, are you?"

"Ah, come on, Doc!"

"He's dead to the world!"

"What about Mrs. Kemmett?"

"She won't be back till morning." Evans grinned. "I've gotten very good at hiding the evidence."

Leon wagged his head in defeat and sat down. "Oh, all right. But just one more, and that's it!"

Five hours later both men were drunk. The doctor was drunker than McMannigle, who'd had only one drink for every two of Evans's, but he was drunker than he should have been while guarding a prisoner. Throwing in his cards with disgust at himself and anger at Evans for luring him into this situation, he shoved back his chair, stood a little unsteadily, and headed for the examining room.

Evans had checked the man's wound several times over the course of the night, but Leon wanted to be reassured the man was still there. Not that he could possibly go anywhere in his condition.

Leon gently twisted the knob and cracked the door. Yes, sir, there he was, God bless him—a long black hump atop the bed at the other side of the dark room, snoring raucously through his open mouth.

"Well, I reckon we'd better call it a night," Evans said, tossing back one last drink. "Remember, Deputy—you're on duty." Standing, he corked the bottle and noticed it was empty. "Oh, Jesus, what if Katherine sees?" he mumbled, tossing the bottle in the trash and stumbling off to his room.

" 'Night, Doc," Leon called dryly. "Thanks ... for everything."

Then he sat down, planted his elbows on the table, and rubbed his face. He yawned and checked his watch. Midnight. Shit. He was tired and drunk and it was going to be one hell of a long time till morning.

How in the hell was he going to stay awake?

Looking around, he saw the book on which Evans's overflowing ashtray was perched. He slipped the volume out from beneath the ashtray and turned it over to read the spine.

The Agememnon of Aeschylus. Huh.

He set the book on the table and turned to page one.

The next thing he knew his head was on the table. Giving a startled grunt, he jerked up and looked around.

The eastern windows were pale, and Evans was walking down the stairs, yawning and smacking his lips.

Leon jumped to his feet, causing his vision to swim and his head to pound. He turned as Evans walked into the room.

"What time is it?" Leon asked him with an air of desperation.

"Around six-thirty," Evans said, running his hands through his sleep-mussed hair. "How'd it go?"

"Christ!" Leon jumped to the door of the examining room and turned the knob. Peering in, he froze, eyes wide.

The bed was vacant, the covers thrown back. The twin lace curtains danced around the open window like wings.

★★★

Stillman and Fay were having breakfast at their kitchen table—scrambled eggs, bacon, fried potatoes, and baking powder biscuits. Both were dressed and ready for the day, having risen earlier than usual so Stillman could get over to Evans's place to relieve Leon.

Stillman ate the last of his eggs and tossed back the last of his coffee. He put his hand on Fay's and gave her a lascivious wink.

"Had fun last night?"

She looked up from the papers she'd been grading while she ate. "A lady and a gentleman do not talk of such things." She smirked.

"Well, you might be a lady, all right, but you sure weren't acting like one last night."

"Nor you a gentleman!" She laughed as he got up and took his plate to the washtub.

"And that's just how I like it," he said, leaning down to kiss her cheek. "I have to go. See you tonight."

"Good-bye, Ben." She kissed his lips. "I love you."

He grabbed his hat off a wall peg and donned it. Heading for the door, he yelled, "Give 'em hell, Teacher!"

"You, too, Sheriff!"

Closing the door behind him, Stillman heard the thunder of a galloping horse. Stopping on the stoop, he looked up at Leon McMannigle approaching on his snorting steeldust.

Stillman's pulse quickened, knowing instantly something was wrong. "What's the matter?" he said as he headed for the gate.

Leon drew up before the picket fence and shook his head. He was breathing hard and his face looked drawn and pale beneath its natural mahogany. "I really messed up bad, Ben."

"What is it?"

"Shambeau. He got away from me."

"How?"

"He slipped out the window up at the doc's place last night. I'm sorry. I let the doc talk me into taking a few drinks, and I fell asleep."

Stillman stood there, his pulse whistling in his ears, trying to pull his thoughts together. He had to admit that part of him rejoiced at the news. The other part—the part that knew he had to bring Shambeau back in—was screaming with exasperation.

He looked at Leon. "Did he get a horse?"

The deputy nodded. "I rode over to the stable first thing. Auld wasn't even there yet, but the barn doors had been jimmied open, and the trapper's horse was gone." He shook his head, wincing as if in physical pain. "I checked out his tracks beneath the window up at the doc's, Ben. He made them hours ago. He's gone with the wind, sure enough!"

"Shit."

"I'm really sorry, Ben. Damnit!"

"Take it easy," Stillman said. "It could've happened to anyone."

"If you want my badge, you got it."

"When I want your badge, I'll ask for it. Why don't you start tracking him? It'll take me awhile to get my horse and gear. No doubt he headed south, so how 'bout if we meet at the south side of Squaw Butte in about an hour?"

"You got it," McMannigle said. He shook his head and stared at Stillman beseechingly.

"Forget about it now," Ben admonished him. "Ride!"

Leon reined his horse around, aimed him south, and put the steel to him. In moments, horse and rider were out of sight

Stillman turned and walked back to the house. Fay stood just inside the door. "What happened?"

Stillman told her.

"Oh, God."

Stillman's sentiments exactly.

CHAPTER TEN

AT THE SOUTH edge of town, Stillman gave Sweets the spurs and galloped along the two-track wagon trail which ambled across the prairie, down ravines, and over hogbacks, toward the Two-Bear Mountains looming before him, their first front showing green-gold in the climbing morning sun.

Squaw Butte was a rocky-topped, copper-colored cone standing above the prairie about four miles south of Clantick, just beyond the brush-choked cut of an unnamed coulee. The coulee ran swift with snowmelt, and Stillman had to find a shallow ford before crossing. Afterward, he spurred Sweets up the other side of the coulee, through juneberry and hawthorn bramble, and across the last hundred yards to the butte.

He found Leon sitting his steeldust on the south side, the deputy's black, flat-brimmed hat tipped against the chill breeze which toyed with his bright red neckerchief and blue plaid mackinaw. The holster containing his Smith & Wesson revolver poked from beneath the coat and was tied by a rawhide thong to his thigh.

"What'd you find?" Stillman asked him.

"I followed his tracks southeast and lost them in a muddy hollow." Leon shook his head. "He's a cagey son of a duck. I just don't see how he's makin' it with that shoulder all torn up. And the damn doc, he promised me the man would be out cold until noon!"

Stillman stared southeastward. "Damn," he muttered.

"I feel just awful about this, Ben."

"I know you do, I know you do. And you're not gonna like what I have to say, but here it is: I want you to go back to town and manage things while I go after him."

"What!"

"You heard me. It could take three or four days to track this man down, and we can't both be away from town that long. I want you to go back and hold down the fort."

"Uh-uh, Ben," Leon protested, wagging his head. "I let the devil get away. I'm tracking him down!"

"I'm all outfitted for several days ride," Stillman said, reaching back and patting his saddlebags. "You don't even have a bedroll on your horse."

"Well, I'll ride back and get one!"

Stillman shook his head. "No, Leon. I want you to watch over the office while I track him."

"Ben, I'm the man who lost him. Besides that, I'm your deputy. I should be goin' after him while you manage the office!"

"I know that, and under normal circumstances I'd let you do it, but I have to go. It has nothing to do with your ability. I hate to pull rank, but that's what I'm doing."

McMannigle stared back at him, his brown forehead creased deep with scowl lines. Finally, the deputy gave a reluctant sigh and shook his head. "Okay," he said. "You're the boss. But you really shouldn't be heading out there alone."

"I don't intend to. I'm gonna see if Jody Harmon will give me a hand."

"Jody?"

"He's lived in those mountains all his life, knows every hoot an' hollow."

"I don't doubt that." A faint humorous glint shone in Leon's eyes. "Think Crystal will let him go—with her havin' a new baby and all?"

Stillman shrugged. "Well, her sister's stayin' with them, so she wouldn't be alone...."

"Jody'd be about as good a guide as you'd find. He's half Indian, too. Might be able to second-guess some of Shambeau's ways and means."

"That's what I'm hoping," Stillman said. He gigged his horse southward and called over his shoulder, "Keep the home fires burnin'."

"You watch your ass, damnit."

Stillman rode down the grade, carpeted with tender green grass shoots and gray-green sage tufts, and hooked up with the main wagon road on the other side of a low hill. As he followed the road southward, he tried to reason out why it was so important to him that he be the one to track Shambeau. He came up with nothing solid.

Did he feel a kinship with the man or feel he knew the

man better than anyone else because he'd known so many others like him?

He wasn't sure. It just felt important, deep down, that he be the one to track him. That, if need be, he be the one to kill him.

***

An hour later he was cantering down the trail leading to the Harmon ranch, the cabin, barn, and corrals of which sat nestled in the buttes along Whitetail Creek. Smoke puffed from the cabin's wide stone chimney, and as Stillman rode through the front gate, he heard the clang of a blacksmith's hammer.

"Hello. It's Ben," he hailed as he brought his horse up to the windmill in the center of the yard.

Nearby, a little blue-eyed boy of about two sat shoveling dust with a wood spoon. He wore a blue wool coat and mittens, but his hood hung down his back and his thin, white curls danced atop his head.

"Well, hello there," Stillman said, leaning down from his saddle to give the lad a friendly grin. "What you got there? A spoon? Well, don't you look as happy as a dog fox in a pullet house!"

The boy looked up at him, a bright-eyed grin spreading across his dirty, pudgy face. He cackled and showed Stillman the spoon.

"Hey, Ben!"

Stillman turned toward the blacksmith shop where

Jody Harmon stood wearing a leather apron and wielding a hammer in one hand, tongs in the other.

"Hello there, young man." Stillman jerked a thumb at the kid playing in the dirt. "Now, I know they grow fast, but this can't be the one Crystal delivered during all that craziness last winter..."

Jody grinned and set the hammer and tongs on the forge, then pulled off his gloves as he stepped out from the blacksmith shop and tucked them inside his apron. He was a stocky young man with straight black hair and a strong, chiseled face. His father, Bill Harmon, had been an Irish frontiersman and Stillman's old hide-hunting pal, and his mother had been a full-blooded Cree from Canada. He picked up the chattering little boy, who was still staring wide-eyed at Stillman.

"No, this is little William Ben's cousin, Luke. Luke, can you say hi to Sheriff Stillman?"

The boy extended the spoon toward Stillman and said, "Ca! Cha-ca-caaaaa!"

"Well, hello to you, too, Luke, and yes, that's one mighty fine lookin' cha-ca-ca."

The child giggled delightedly.

Stillman laughed. Jody held up his hand for Ben to shake. "How you doin', Sheriff?"

"Not very well, I'm afraid."

"Oh? Light and come on for a cup of coffee and tell me about it."

***

Inside, the kitchen smelled of diapers and warm milk.

Jody's wife, Crystal, sat in the rocking chair beside the range. She'd been nursing the tiny baby in her arms and was now pulling her blouse down to cover her bosoms.

"Oh, sorry, Crystal," Stillman said, flushing, stopping suddenly, and averting his gaze.

Crystal, a pretty blond tomboy who'd grown up in these mountains just as Jody had, gave a husky laugh. "Oh, come on in, Ben—unless you're shy around exposed teats. I was just finishing up nursing little William Ben here, but I'm liable to start again just as soon as he starts bawling for it."

"She will, too, Ben," Jody said, cutting his eyes at Stillman. "That girl doesn't have one ounce of modesty."

"That's what childbirth does to a girl," Crystal carped.

To Ben, Jody said, "I've known her all her life. She's never had a modest bone in her body."

Crystal's eyes flashed boldly, with a hint of licentiousness. "I've never known you to complain." She grinned.

Jody flushed and just shook his head. Stillman pegged his hat on the wall. Chuckling—he'd long ago grown accustomed to the couple's back-and-forth banter—he headed for Crystal and kissed her cheek.

"How you doin', girl?"

"Well, I'd tell you how I keep getting the crying fits for no reason and that my titties feel like I've been suckling bobcats, but my husband would chide me for bein' immodest"

Jody snorted as he poured a cup of coffee from the big black percolator on the range. "Ben, you know Crystal's sister, Marie."

Stillman turned from Crystal and the baby. He hadn't realized anyone else was in the room, but now he saw the blond woman, a few years older than Crystal, standing back by the well pump, a tin cup of oatmeal in her hand. Chin drooped toward her chest, she seemed to be hiding in the shadows. While Marie shared Crystal's blond hair and pretty, blue-eyed face, that was the extent of their resemblance.

Marie was a mousy little thing—shy and always deferring. When she spoke to others besides Crystal, it was with a soft child's voice, as though she were afraid of something unseen or felt she never quite measured up.

But that wasn't surprising in light of the man she'd married—a drunk, abusive cuss named Ivan Wheatly. It had taken Crystal a good long time, but she'd finally rescued Marie and her four kids away from the man. That's why she was here now, living with Jody and Crystal until she could figure out a new life for herself and her family.

"Marie," Stillman said with a gracious smile and nod. "How are you?"

"Oh, I'm... gettin' along," she said with a nervous little laugh, unable to meet Stillman's friendly gaze. Clipping off the opportunity for further conversation, she moved quickly to Crystal, to whom she handed the oatmeal.

"Thanks, sis," Crystal said.

"Is that hot enough?"

"It's good."

"Not too hot?"

"No, it's perfect, Marie," Crystal said. "Why don't you pour yourself a cup of coffee and sit at the table with Ben and Jody?"

"Oh, no," Marie said in her little girl's voice, moving toward little Luke, who sat chattering on the braided rug before the living room hearth. "Me and Luke'll just stay over here, out of everyone's way."

She picked up the child and sat in the overstuffed chair in front of the popping, sizzling fire.

"Where's the rest of your brood, Marie?" Stillman asked, trying to engage the woman in conversation.

Her nervous eyes flitted to Jody's as if he could answer the question better than she. "Oh, they're ... outside with their guns, aren't they Jody?"

"Rabbit hunting," Jody said with a smile. "They're gettin' to be quite the shots, those boys. They've taken over my job of puttin' meat on the table."

"Yes, they're... good boys," Marie said, lowering her head to gently kiss Luke's cheek, effectively ending her involvement in the conversation. Jody sipped his coffee and turned to Stillman, who sat at one end of the long kitchen table, brooding into his own coffee mug. "Well, I can see in your face you have trouble, Ben."

"I can, too," Crystal said with a sympathetic expression. "What's wrong? It isn't Fay, is it?"

"No, Fay's well," Stillman said. "I have a professional problem, you might say." He looked at Jody. "I was wondering if I could steal you away from these ladies for a couple days—two or three, maybe more. I need your tracking skills."

Jody looked at Crystal, who looked back at him. To Ben, Jody said, "Tell me about it, Sheriff."

Stillman told him the story, beginning with Shambeau's

rampage in the woodcutters' shack and ending with the trapper's escape the night before when he should have been sleeping off Doc Evans's ether.

"You think he headed back to his cabins?" Jody asked.

"All we know is he headed south into the Two-Bears," Stillman said. "Which makes me think yes, he probably headed back to one of his cabins—wherever in the hell that might be. I've heard he's pretty secretive about where he lives."

Jody was rubbing his jaw and staring out the window, pondering the situation. "Probably headed for Timber Creek."

"What's that?" Stillman said.

"He had a place on Timber Creek. Just a dugout"

Stillman raised a surprised brow. "You know that?"

"I stumbled onto it one time when me and Pa were hunting that way. Saw Louis out stretching hides. I don't think he saw us, and we left him alone. We both knew what a loner he was even back then—ten years ago, at least"

"You think the cabin's still there?"

"I don't know, but it's worth a shot. It's probably the closest one to town. I think the other two or three are farther out in the Missouri river breaks. They'd be damn near impossible to find. Like lookin' for a needle in a haystack. That's a big, woolly country out there."

"Do you think you could find this place?"

Jody looked at Crystal as if for permission. "I could try."

Crystal did not look pleased. She frowned at her husband fearfully.

"Crystal, Ben needs my help," Jody said.

"Crystal," Stillman said, "you say the word and I'll hightail it out of here—alone. I know you have the baby and all, an'—"

"Oh, he'll be restless as a tomcat if he doesn't go," Crystal groused. To Stillman, she said, "But you have to promise me, Sheriff, you won't let him get hurt."

"You have my promise," Stillman said. "I just need him to get me to Louis's first cabin. The arrest I'll handle myself."

Jody was already on his feet He pecked his wife and baby on their cheeks and said, "Thanks, honey," and hurried off for his gear.

Stillman sat at the table and sipped his coffee. Crystal was staring at him with pursed lips and knit brows. Feeling cowed, Stillman winced and turned his gaze to the window.

CHAPTER ELEVEN

TOMMY FALK WOKE that morning with a brain-splitting headache that began with the burn at the top of his head—oh, it felt like he'd been doused with kerosene and set aflame!—and that hammered rail spikes deep within his skull, all the way to his jaw.

It hurt so bad that as he lay on his bunk grinding his teeth, he almost felt like calling out for his mother; that needling, teetotaler devil he'd left with his worthless lout of a so-called father in Silver Springs, Iowa. He wasn't in that bad of a shape, though. Hell, just the image of her wooden smile and cow-stupid eyes that had always been buried in her ten-pound Bible, even when Tommy came home sucking on candy he'd stolen from the crossroads mercantile, made his head hurt even worse.

"Get up, kid," a voice said, breaking into his misery. "Your turn for woodsplittin', and I need some pronto."

It was the cook. Jack Hanson, who stood at the big Circle range slicing sidepork into a pan.

"Send someone else out to do it. Can't you see I'm hurtin'?"

"You weren't hurtin' too bad to ride into town yesterday and drink your fill of whiskey, so get out there."

"That's about all I can do is drink whiskey," the kid grouched, throwing his legs to the floor and squeezing his eyes shut against the Apache war clubs thumping his brain. "It takes the pain away... sort of."

"What's the problem, kid?" Donny Olnan called from the back of the bunkhouse, shaving at one of the two mirrors tacked to the wall. The other ten men were either shaving or dressing or scrubbing out their armpits, cigarettes or cigars drooping from their lips. "You got a headache?"

"That's real funny," Falk groaned as he stepped into his pants. "You're a real cutup, Donny. You just wait till I'm feelin' well again. Then let's you and me take a walk out to the trash heap with our six-shooters strapped to our thighs." The kid cursed and buckled his belt, his nose wrinkled with pure disdain, the kind of anger he normally would have acted on had his head not felt like shattered glass. "Then we'll see who's so funny."

Squeals and laughter.

"Take it easy, kid. Remember what the deputy said in town yesterday. There's folks back East makin' real nice head rugs." Aver Wilkinson elbowed Bernie Phipps standing beside him gargling whiskey. "Why, one o' those fine young lassies over at Mrs. Lee's place could run her titties through it all day and never know it belonged to a horse!"

Wilkinson guffawed and Bernie Phipps sprayed his mouthful of whiskey at the window.

"That's real damn funny," the kid said, mooning as he

pulled on his sheepskin and hat and headed for the door.

"Oh, come on, Tommy, don't get your hair all in a kink!" someone else quipped as Falk slammed the door on the ensuing laughter.

Pine and aspen logs were stacked along the bunkhouse wall near the door. Falk grabbed one off the stack, set it on the chopping block, and picked up the splitter. As he brought the iron maul down through the stout aspen chunk, he imagined doing the same thing to the face of Louis Shambeau. He'd never seen the man's face close up before—things had happened too fast that night in the cabin for the kid to even have glanced at the trapper's mug—but he imagined what it would look like just before the wedge hit. He imagined the man drawing thick, wet lips back and begging for his life.

"No, Tommy, no! Please! I didn't mean—!"

The wedge came down again with a thunk, the log splitting cleanly, the two halves flying in opposite directions, and the splitter sinking a good two inches into the chopping block.

"Sorry, half-breed," Falk muttered, inhaling loudly as the tender nerve endings in his scalp—or what remained of it—wailed like wounded wolves. "Just a little dose of Falk's justice—frontier style!"

"Hey, Tommy, can we see it?"

The voice seemed to come out of nowhere. Falk stopped what he was doing and turned to see three horseback drovers grinning down at him. Tommy had been so wrapped up in his vengeance fantasy he hadn't heard them ride up—Lazy R riders from over east

Falk scowled. "What the hell do you boys want?"

"We were just riding back from town—had the day off yesterday so we spent it over at Mrs. Lee's," Roy Long explained with a grin, "and we were wonderin' if we could see it"

Falk's scowl lines deepened beneath the red bandanna stretched taut across his skull. "See it?"

"Your head," one of the other men said. "Ain't none of us ever seen a scalped noggin before."

"I heard of a man scalped by Comanch down in Texas, but no, I ain't never seen one alive," another said.

Falk was exasperated. "What the hell do you think I am?" he spat his face turning as red as the bandanna. "A damn *circus show!*"

"Well, hell, you could just give us a peek," the third man said, his face scrunched imploringly around a big, brushy mustache and ragged goatee. "The trapper make all them bumps on your face, too?"

Tommy just stared at the men, so angry his blood was steaming in his veins and threatening to burst through his pores. He stepped forward, wielding the splitter in both hands. "Get the heck out of here, you—!"

His tirade was cut off by the bunkhouse door opening behind him and several of his comrades pouring out with grins on their faces.

"Hey, if it ain't the lazy Lazy R boys!" the cook, Jack Hanson, bellowed. "Hidee, Slim, Roy, Mike! Light an' sit a spell. I'd offer you a cup of coffee if young Falk here would quit draggin' his ass and split me some wood!"

"Ah, that's okay, Jack," Roy said. "We were just stoppin'

by to see if the kid'd show us his noggin, but he's just plain owly this mornin'.'"

"Oh, come on, Tom"—one of the other Bar 7 riders nudged Falk's side—"take your bandanna off and show the boys."

"Diddle yourself, Milt!"

Laughs all around. Tommy stood there wielding the maul like he was about to take it to each man in turn.

"Yeah, he's just plain ornery till he's had his red eye," Jack Hanson explained. "Best just to leave him alone. You sure you boys won't come on inside? We could sure use some fresh conversation around here."

"Nah, we best get on back to the Lazy R," Slim Wilbur said. "Like we told Tommy, we had yesterday off, so we spent it in town at Mrs. Lee's." He gave a coyote hoot, his wide mouth slashing his face practically in two. "But we're due back this mornin' to bring the herd down close to the headquarters—for calvin' and brandin' and all."

"Well, stop back when you can stay."

"We'll sure do that," Slim said as he and the others touched their hatbrims and reined their mounts away. Slim stopped, frowning, and turned back. "Oh, say, did you boys hear the news about Shambeau?"

"What news?" Tommy snarled.

"He got away from the deputy up at the doc's place last night."

"Say what!"

"Sure enough." Slim nodded seriously. "He went and slipped out the doc's window in the middle of the night. Stillman's after him now. Auld over at the livery said the man broke in and stole his horse out, then headed south into the Two-Bears."

"Damn!" carped the Bar 7 rider called Condor Dave because his face owned a distinctly raptorial nose and eyes.

Falk just stood there, eyes slitted, not saying anything, wielding the splitter as though he were still wanting to use it on the visitors.

"I can't believe those morons let him get away," the Bar 7 foreman said through gritted teeth. "After what he done to Jackson and Mueller!"

"Those two tin-plated jailers couldn't keep a baby in a bassinet!" Roy Long exclaimed.

"I always thought they were good lawmen," Hanson said wonderingly. "I mean, they tamed Clantick. And Stillman, hell, he was one of the best marshals the frontier ever seen!"

"Maybe he's gettin' old and losin' his touch," one of the Bar 7 men opined.

Roy Long said, "I don't know—if I was you boys, I'd give ole Stillman a hand. He ain't never gonna find Shambeau. Hell, Louis's probably already back on the Missouri by now, planning his next kill."

Roy jerked his horse around to follow the other riders through the gate. "Be seein' you boys. If Stillman don't catch that maniac, let me know, will you—so's I can get my hair cropped good and close!"

With that, Roy Long galloped his horse through the gate and back onto the trail, heading east.

Falk turned to the tall foreman, Dave Groom, who stood staring after the Lazy R riders in his denim shirt and suspenders, thoughtfully sucking a cigarette with his Stetson tipped back on his head.

"Did you hear that, Dave?" Falk said. "Shambeau's on the loose. I don't know about you, but—"

"Hold on, hold on, kid," Groom growled. "I'll go talk to the old man." Groom started toward the main house. Over his shoulder, he called, "You boys get back inside and pad out your bellies."

"We gotta go after him, Dave!" Falk yelled. "He took my *hair!*"

Groom mounted the veranda and knocked on the door. When a man yelled, "Come!" Groom removed his hat and opened the door.

In the kitchen to his left, the Hendricks family—Mr. and Mrs. and the two daughters—were sitting at the table, working on breakfast, a big speckled coffeepot sitting on a wood trivet before them. Seeing the pot, Groom's mouth watered, for Hanson's lack of stove wood had prevented him from brewing coffee.

Hendricks's back was to Groom, and he craned his neck around to see behind him. "What is it, Dave?"

"A couple of Lazy R riders were just here and left," Groom said.

"Oh? Come on in and pour a cup of coffee."

"Don't mind if I do," Groom said.

As he moved toward the table, one of the girls, with whom Groom had shared several private moments in the lean-to shack off the south barn, gave him a lascivious wink. Blushing, Groom quickly turned his eyes to Mrs. Hendricks and nodded an affable greeting.

"Megan, get Mr. Groom a cup," Mrs. Hendricks told the daughter.

"Certainly, Mother."

While the girl went to the cupboard for a cup, Hendricks said, "So, what is it, Dave? Our beeves been mixing with theirs again?"

"No, sir, that's not it," Groom said.

He paused as Megan came around behind him and, brushing against his arm, handed him the cup. Groom glanced quickly at the parents, but the eyes of both were on their plates. The other daughter, however, saw it all, and snickered into her hand.

Groom jerked an angry look at Megan, who gave him a wink and returned to her chair.

"What is it, Rachel?" Mrs. Hendricks asked the snickering daughter.

"Oh, nothing, Mother."

"These girls do not know how to behave around men, Walt," Mrs. Hendricks chided her husband. "In the future, I hope you'll meet your foreman out on the veranda. The house must be off-limits to the help."

"Yes, of course, dear," Hendricks said with an air of impatience. He turned to Groom. "So, Dave, what's the problem?"

Groom sipped his coffee to cover his embarrassment. "It's Shambeau, Mr. Hendricks. The Lazy R boys say he got away from Stillman and McMannigle, and he's heading back into the mountains."

Mrs. Hendricks looked sharply at her husband. "Walt!"

With a weary sigh, Hendricks threw his napkin on his half-empty plate and shoved his chair back. Standing, he said, "Guess this ain't for the females, Dave. Let's continue this discussion on the porch," and headed for the door.

Outside. Groom, who had held on to his coffee cup, sidled up to his boss. Hendricks was staring off toward the corrals and blacksmith shop. "So, he's on the loose, eh?"

"Yes, sir."

"And I suppose the rest of the men heard about it."

"Yes, sir."

"I suppose *Falk* heard about it."

"Yes, sir, he did at that."

"And I suppose they're wanting to go after him themselves, that it?"

Groom nodded. "Well, sir, that maniac did make off with the kid's hair, and he did kill poor ole Jackson and Mueller. If we don't stick up for our own boys, boss, you know—"

"Yeah, I know, I know," Hendricks groused, nodding angrily. "If we don't stick up for our own men, it can be damn hard on morale."

"That's about how it works, sir. They'll ride for the brand as long as—"

"I know, Dave, I know—as long as the brand rides for them."

"Yes, sir, Mr. Hendricks."

Hendricks stood there for a long time, working the bacon from his teeth with his tongue and thinking it over. Finally, he turned to his foreman. "All right, Dave. Have them saddled up and ready to ride in half an hour. Leave a few here to keep up with the chores around the headquarters in case any calves start dropping."

"Yes, sir, Mr. Hendricks."

"And tell those left behind to stay away from the damn house, Dave."

"I'll tell them, sir."

"And Dave?" Hendricks looked at the tall, good-looking foreman, askance.

"Yes, Mr. Hendricks?"

"You haven't been doing anything... indecorous... with either of my daughters, have you?"

Groom swallowed and nearly choked on his tongue. He shook his head with vehemence. "No, sir, Mr. Hendricks!"

Hendricks watched his foreman for several seconds, then his eyes relaxed and he nodded. "Okay, Dave. See to the men."

"You got it, boss!"

Groom handed Hendricks his empty cup and headed for the bunkhouse, his heart pounding harder than it had when he'd had Megan Hendricks bent over the tack bench.

CHAPTER TWELVE

AT HIGH NOON Doc Evans walked down the board-walk on First Street and turned into Sam Wa's Café. He stood near the door, twisting the ends of his waxed red mustache and scouring the room for a table.

Sam's, as usual at this hour, was hopping with business-men, cowboys, railroaders, and soldiers from Fort Assini-boine. Evans usually tried to get here by eleven forty-five to beat the crowd, but he'd had to relocate the dislocated knee of a telegraph lineman.

"This way, Doc," Evelyn Vincent said as she walked past him with a crooked finger. "Just cleared a little table back here against the wall," she continued as Evans followed her through the crowd. "Maybe we'll be able to keep you out of trouble back here."

The waitress snorted dryly as Evans sat down.

"Trouble? *Me?*" the doctor said, feigning a wide-eyed look of innocence. He knew that by now it had probably gotten around town and halfway around the county that he'd gotten Leon McMannigle drunk last night and thus less capable of performing his duties as efficiently as was expected of one of the top five sheriff's deputies in the territory.

"Trouble? Most certainly you," the waitress returned. "Everyone knows Leon wouldn't normally drink on duty, Doc. Not only have you embarrassed him before the whole town, you have him feeling about knee-high to a grasshopper! Now, what'll it be? If you haven't noticed, I have quite a few mouths to feed."

When Evans had ordered his usual hamburger with fried onions and fried potatoes and gravy, Evelyn stomped back toward the kitchen, weaving her way through the tables. Evans crossed his arms on the table and glanced around, noticing several disapproving looks aimed his way.

He frowned and dropped his gaze, chagrined. He knew he shouldn't have enticed the deputy into imbibing last night, but Evans rarely had company except for Katherine Kemmett, and the woman was an incorruptible, irredeemable teetotaler. A man could literally die of thirst in the presence of such a prude! Due to Katherine's perpetual hovering, he himself hadn't had but one or two drinks in a night in weeks; he'd just taken the opportunity of Leon's presence to oil his tonsils.

Can't blame him, for God's sakes. After all, he did live out in the middle of friggin' nowhere, getting paid in hay and chickens for skills he'd acquired in one of the finest medical schools in the East! Not only that, but his only female companion these days was a prim and proper minister's widow.

Speak of the devil!

Mrs. Kemmett walked purposefully past the window

and turned into the café. She looked around the room. Spying him, she started his way. As she came, Evans watched her, and in spite of his previous sentiment, he found himself admiring the figure she cut beneath all that cotton and crinoline. She was heavy-bosomed in spite of the tight corset she wore, flat-bellied, and round-hipped. And there was just something about all that prim and proper prudishness, all that church-pew varnish and gloss, that kept him, a veteran whoremonger, beguiled and imagining how it would be, unbuttoning all those buttons, unfastening all those fasteners...

"When I didn't find you at home, I figured you'd be here," she said as she approached, removing her long, white gloves. He could tell by her castigating tone that she, too, had gotten the news.

"Yes, I decided to stop by for a bite but rather wish I'd stayed at the house." He scowled and glanced furtively across the room.

She sat in the chair across from him. "Yes, as well you should have. A man of your ilk should stay as close to his own yard as possible, lest he get egged and stoned for his transgressions, of which there are plenty."

"He didn't have to drink!"

"Oh, Clyde!"

"Just because I was drinking—for the first time in weeks, I might add; even Christ deserved a bender in the desert for God's sakes!—didn't mean he had to imbibe."

"Such talk! And I suppose you did all you could to discourage him... ?"

Evans fidgeted like one of Katherine's Sunday-schoolers caught drinking communion wine in die rectory.

"Oh, Clyde! What are we going to do with you?"

"Yes, that's the question, isn't it?" Evelyn Vincent said as she set the doctor's meal on the table before him. She looked at Katherine. "Do you want me to find you another table, Mrs. Kemmett? Those railroaders over there should be leaving in a minute."

Katherine sighed, crossed her hands on the table, and looked Evans over critically. "No, I think I'd better stay here and give counsel... as best I can."

"Good luck."

"Oh, help me," Evans moaned.

When Katherine had ordered her usual bowl of soup and buttered roll, Evelyn headed back toward the kitchen. She stopped halfway across the room to accept a tip and field a flirtation. When she turned away with an affable smile, she saw three strange men enter the cafe, look around, and head for the table the railroaders were vacating.

She gave the men a cursory appraisal, noting they were strangers. Only half-consciously deciding she did not like how they looked, she headed for the kitchen and the several orders awaiting her there.

***

Behind her, the three strangers made their way to the table, walking stiffly and appraising the crowd with the skeptical, defensive scrutiny of outsiders. The one in the lead, who wore a frock coat over a paisley vest and a black slouch hat with hammered silver around the crown, mistook Evelyn's unfavorable appraisal for a favorable one, and studied her backside as she disappeared through the batwing to the kitchen.

As he threw the tail of his coat back and sat down, he grinned at the other two men. "Pretty," he said. "Did you see the way she looked at me?"

"Who?" Newt Jarvis asked. He was a big, mustached man in an ill-fitting suit.

"The waitress. I think she likes me."

The third man, Calvin Whitehead, chuckled. "Hell, Blade, you think they all like you!"

The man in the frock coat, whose name was Bledin Carstairs, leaned toward Whitehead with a self-satisfied grin, slapped the table lightly with his pinky-ringed right hand, and said, "That's because they do, my boy. They do!"

"Why don't we forget about the girls?" Jarvis said. "You can diddle all the girls you want after we've pulled the bank job over in Shelby."

Carstairs glanced around coolly, then sat back in his chair and looked at Jarvis. "Why don't you talk a little louder, Jarv? I don't think those two against the wall quite heard the whole thing."

"Nobody can hear nothin' in this crowd," Jarvis said.

"We're strangers," Carstairs retorted. "People in little towns scrutinize strangers—haven't you seen all the eyes that have turned our way since we walked in here? They also like to eavesdrop. So, keep your damn voice down or I'll put you right back on the train you just crawled off of, you big buffoon, and send you back to Dakota where you belong."

Calvin Whitehead, the youngest of the trio who was dressed much like Carstairs but with noticeably cheaper tailoring, leaned over the table to regard both men with an acquiescent glance. "Come on, gentlemen, settle down. Don't get your tails all in a hook. We got a job to discuss."

The three men quickly formed smiles as the waitress approached looking harried, her smooth cheeks flushed and her blond hair falling out of its bun. "Gentlemen," she said by way of cool greeting, "what will it be?"

Bledin Carstairs blinked his flirtatious eyes and unconsciously widened his arms, edging his coat lapels back so the girl could get a good look at the gold watch chain looping out from a pocket of his lavish vest. "Hello there, pretty lady." His voice was deep and silky, like warm spring water bubbling over gumbo.

"Yes sir, what'll it be?" the young woman asked with an impatient sigh, giving a glance to the room which, while beginning to thin, was still aswarm with hungry diners.

"How 'bout a stroll along the river later?"

Evelyn sighed again, this time with real annoyance. She didn't mind men flirting with her—it all came with the job—but when she ran across a particularly persistent flirt during the noon or suppertime rush, one so self-centered as to believe she had all the time in the world to entertain him and him alone, she wanted to draw a pistol and start shooting.

Apparently, her face adequately conveyed her mood. The man, flushing slightly, asked for the lunch special, and the others followed suit. Smiling a little too brightly, Evelyn swung around and headed for the kitchen, unaware her bottom was getting another long, slow appraisal by Bledin Carstairs.

"Yeah, she's real crazy for you, Blade," big Jarvis snickered, nervously smoothing his unruly mustache with a hammy paw.

"Hey, the poor girl's busy," Whitehead said. "Even if she did have eyes for him, she wouldn't have time to flirt."

"Ah, the voice of reason," Carstairs said, sliding his eyes to young Whitehead. He frowned as another thought displaced the image of the waitress's ass. "Where in the hell did you get that suit, anyway?"

"Cheyenne—why?"

"It's ugly."

"It ain't ugly. Besides, it's all I had money for."

"What'd you do with all the money we took—?" Carstairs stopped himself abruptly and glanced around. Lowering his voice, he said, "With all the money from the assay office down in Deadwood?"

Jarvis laughed. "I bet that was gone the day after we split up!" He put a hand on young Whitehead's shoulder and gave him a playful shove. "You know how that little French devil over to Julesburg has him tied to her garter straps!"

Whitehead frowned, annoyed, and said through gritted teeth, "Shut up, Newt! I told you, if you don't have anything good to say about Julieanna, don't say anything at all!"

"You should have wired me for money, kid," Carstairs told him, keeping his voice below the din of the loud conversations surrounding him. "We're supposed to look like professional salesmen, not snake-oil drummers."

Whitehead was churlish. "I do look professional!"

"You look like a snake-oil drummer," Carstairs looked at Newt Jarvis and shook his head.

"I do?" Whitehead said. "What about him?"

"Hey!" Jarvis growled mock angrily.

Carstairs appraised big Jarvis and laughed. "Newt could crawl into the fanciest suit hand-sewn in New York City and still look like just what he is—an ole Missouri mule skinner!" He bent forward, laughing.

Jarvis grinned and yanked on his lapels. "Yeah, I reckon they don't make suits for men my size." He wagged his head sadly. "It still set me back three good drinkin' nights in Bismarck, it did."

"Let's get down to business," Calvin Whitehead said, turning to Carstairs. "You set a date yet, Blade?"

"Well, I did, but that was before last night. Last night something happened right here in Clantick that makes me think we should stick around here for a while."

Jarvis had been about to light a fat cigar. Now he frowned and leaned forward over the lantern in the center of the table. "Wait a minute—I thought you said you didn't want to pull anything here on account of the badass sheriff in town."

"I did," Jarvis said. "But he got called out of town on

business last night. Some—" He stopped abruptly when Jarvis made a slashing motion with his hand. The waitress came up from behind Carstairs and set a bowl of chili and a ham sandwich before him, then went around and set the same meals before the other two men.

"Coffee?" she asked.

"If you wouldn't mind, beautiful lady," Carstairs said with a toothy grin.

"Comin' right up."

Carstairs waited until the waitress had returned with their coffee and left before continuing. "As I was saying, some prisoner escaped the doctor's house last night and headed into the Two-Bear Mountains. Apparently, the man's a trapper who knows his way around the mountains pretty well. So Stillman—that's the sheriff—will probably be occupied for several days."

Whitehead was chewing a mouthful of beefy chili. "So, what do you have in mind?"

"The bank here in town," Carstairs said, taking a bite from his sandwich.

"Isn't there a deputy?" Jarvis asked.

"Yeah, but I think we're okay. He's the one the prisoner escaped from. Apparently, he's not much of a lawman. Word is—I got most of this from some railroad men during breakfast over in the Boston Hotel—that he was drinking when he should have been guarding the trapper." Carstairs grinned. "Also—get this—he's a nigger."

Jarvis looked at Carstairs with surprise. "No kiddin'?"

"Sure enough. Who else they gonna get this far off the

beaten path to play deputy to a hardass like Stillman? Some yessuh, nosuh guy, no doubt. Probably even more of a slacker than usual when his boss is out of town."

Whitehead was busy eating, for he'd been on the train for several days and hadn't had much money for anything but biscuits. "You seen this guy, Blade—this deputy?"

"No, I just got here yesterday. But I really don't think he'll be anything to worry about. And have you seen this town? It's grown by leaps and bounds since I was through here last. Two mercantiles, a livery barn, a damn fancy hotel for this deep in the sticks. And I seen some ranchers in town last night driving leather-seated buggies with brass fittings and the whole shebang!" Carstairs shook his head. "That bank—the First Stockmen's—has to be splitting at the seams. It's the only one in town, one of only three in the whole damn county."

"Well, what in the hell are we doin' here, then?" Jarvis asked.

"Yeah," Whitehead put in after he'd swallowed some coffee. "You always told us it wasn't smart to hole up in the same town you're sizin' up for a strike."

"Well, I didn't know until I got off the train yesterday we were sizin' it up for a strike," Carstairs said testily from behind his coffee cup. The two soldiers sitting behind them had gotten up to leave, and Carstairs watched them askance.

None of the three men said anything until the soldiers had left.

"So, what do we do now, Blade?" young Whitehead asked.

"Well, it's really too late to leave now. I say we just try to make ourselves as inconspicuous as possible while we spend the next couple days sizing things up. I have a room over at the Boston. We'll bunk together there. I've already told the manager two of my, ahem, colleagues were on their way, and we'd be bunking together to save the company some cash."

"Okay," Jarvis said, straightening up and inspecting his attire. "The Boston it is. Sounds slicker'n a schoolmarm's knee." He stretched an arm out and nudged young Whitehead playfully.

"More coffee, boys?" the waitress asked, pot in hand.

Blade looked around and saw that the crowd had thinned considerably. That was probably why the waitress seemed so much more relaxed, not to mention friendly.

"How could I resist such an offer from such a lovely young temptress as yourself?" he said, extending his cup with flair.

The waitress, to his surprise, smiled broadly and even blushed.

"What are you doing tonight, if I may ask, milady?" Carstairs inquired as the young woman freshened his partners' coffee.

"Well, tonight I'll be busy as a bee," she said, smiling. Whitehead and Jarvis snickered and cut their mocking eyes at Carstairs.

"Oh, really?" Carstairs groaned theatrically. "Pray tell this starstruck, heartsick suitor-to-be."

"Well, first I have to wash my hair, then I have to wash my work dresses."

More chuckles from Carstairs's partners.

They settled down considerably, however, when the

girl, lifting the pot from Whitehead's cup, smiled lavishly at Carstairs and said, "But tomorrow night I'm free as the breeze. What'd you have in mind?"

CHAPTER THIRTEEN

"HOLD UP A minute, Ben."

Stillman reined his big bay to a halt and looked behind him. Jody was approaching from a depression in the trail they were following through a wide, grassy valley just behind the first front of the Two-Bears.

"What is it?" Stillman asked the young man.

Jody wore a sheepskin coat, leather gloves, and a cream plainsman strapped to his chin with a horsehair thong and acom fastener. He was appraising the mountain rising on their right

"This valley gets deeper the farther we follow it east. We should get out now. We need to be on the other side of this mountain. Then we can follow Aspen Valley southeast. It's a shortcut toward the river breaks."

"You know these mountains a hell of a lot better than I do," Stillman said. "Lead the way."

"Come on, Dex," Jody said to his horse, urging the buckskin off the trail they'd been following and up the mountain, through low-growing shrubs and over a scattering of black talus. "There's a pretty good switchbacking game trail up here, Ben."

Stillman kneed Sweets up the side of the mountain, following about twenty yards behind Jody. It was a steep climb but the footing after the shale was fairly good, for deer and elk had cut a seven-inch trail in the short grass and gravel-carpeted limestone.

On the ridge Stillman kneed his horse alongside Jody, who sat his saddle staring out over a deep valley filled with conifers and aspens. The buds on the aspens were swollen, preparing to open in a week or two. Ragged snow patches lingered on the south-facing slope. Down the middle of the valley, a stream curved over rocks, slicing a thin wedge between forested slopes. Shunting, puffy clouds swept the terrain with shadows.

"I wonder who stacked those," Stillman said, pointing to a mound of rocks a few yards down the ridge.

"I did," Jody said. "In Pa's memory. This was his favorite place in the Two-Bears. We hunted here a lot. Mostly, though, he'd just sit right there, where I stacked those rocks after he died, and stare out over the valley while he sent me on for the deer or elk we were tracking." He chuckled.

"That was Bill," Stillman said, remembering his old hide hunting pal. "He had a poetic soul."

"Ma's laid out, in the Cree way, on the other ridge, about a half mile east. You can't see the tree from here, but it's a big, lightning-split cottonwood that formed another leader after the split and grew even stouter than before. Ma would've appreciated that."

"No doubt she does, son."

"The Indians believed the spirits of those who've passed return to their favorite places in life and give their blessing."

Stillman thought about this as he moved his eyes up from the rock cairn to the other ridge, eastward, then back to the cairn again. "I reckon I can feel old Bill watching us right now," he said. "I sure miss the old cuss."

Jody didn't say anything.

"Some men leave the world a little worse than before they got here, and some men leave it a little better. Your old man left it better, but it's darker, too, since he went." Stillman looked at Jody and smiled. "He'd be right proud of that grandson of his."

"I think he would." The boy backhanded a tear from his cheek.

Stillman smiled again then started Sweets down the ridge past the cairn.

They rested the horses in the valley, watering them at the creek. The water was cold with snowmelt, giving an instant headache, and the men filled their canteens before heading westward, following the curving trail through the draw. They crossed a saddle and found themselves in Aspen Valley, heading south.

By this time the sun had slipped behind the peaks, and Jody and Stillman began looking for a camping spot.

"Hey," Stillman said as they rode slowly toward a bald mountainside strewn with boulders and scrubby, wind-twisted pines, "I smell smoke."

"Too wet for a forest fire," Jody said.

Stillman worked his nose, scowling. "No, that's camp smoke."

Sniffing it, too, Jody whipped an anxious look at the sheriff. "You don't think it's him, do you?"

"Can't imagine it. But that smoke belongs to someone."

"Where's it coming from?"

Stillman pointed down the draw, westward from where they'd been going to camp. He kneed his horse in that direction and said, "Keep behind me."

"I'm armed," Jody said.

"I don't care," Stillman told him, keeping his voice low. "I promised Crystal I'd bring you back unharmed, and that's exactly what I'm going to do."

"I can take care of myself."

Stillman stopped and tossed the young man a look that would have wilted a cactus.

"All right, all right," young Harmon grouched, lifting his hands and falling back.

Stillman rode across the bowl to the conifers on its north-facing side. Staying close to the trees, knowing he'd be hard to spot against them, he rode slowly eastward.

The wind funneling toward him brought with it the smell of burning pine. Reaching behind, he shucked his Henry sixteen-shot repeater from his saddleboot, quietly levered a round in the chamber, and rode on.

When he came to a bend in the game trail he was following, hugging a spring freshet lined with rocks, he dismounted and tied Sweets to a low branch. The smell of the smoke was strengthening, which meant the camp was close and getting closer.

Thoughtfully patting the horse's rear, he lifted his rifle and walked on.

He stopped when he saw a thin column of smoke rising from behind several large rocks, and turned into the trees, making a wide circle around the camp, then walking back north, toward the clearing.

Several stumps and deadfalls blocked his view of the camp. He made his way slowly to a large stump, stepping carefully across the leaf-and-branch-littered forest floor, and crouched, listening.

Hearing nothing but the popping of a small fire, his heartbeat quickened. Could he have found Shambeau? It seemed unlikely, but maybe the man's injured shoulder had slowed him up and caused him to make an early camp. Hell, maybe his sutures had ruptured and he was bleeding....

Cautiously Stillman moved out from behind the deadfall and around a boulder, turning sharply into the camp and bringing his rifle shoulder high.

"Hold it!"

He froze, blinking and frowning at the two young men—boys, really—hunkered on a deadfall log before a dying fire. Both were dressed in homespun breeches and hide coats. The clothes looked worn and shabby—probably old hand-me-downs—and the boys' deerskin mittens and wool hats were threadbare and filled with holes.

The boys appeared even more surprised to see Stillman than Stillman was to see them. Giving a start, both shrank back on the log, eyeing Stillman's rifle fearfully.

"Please, mister," one of them said, his teeth chattering. "Don't shoot!"

Stillman quickly lowered the rifle and held out his hand, palm out. "It's all right, boys. I'm not going to shoot."

Stillman looked around for sign of grown-ups or horses and saw nothing. Not even any blankets or camping supplies. It was just these two boys—aged about ten and twelve by the looks of them—and a small fire set in a hole they must have carved out of the ground with their hands. Their wood supply was almost gone—only a few twigs torn from a dead cottonwood branch lying beside the hole.

"What are you two doing here?"

The oldest boy, who had auburn hair cut straight across his forehead, said, "We were out huntin' and our horse spooked yesterday an' threw me and Robert off. Thunder run away and we couldn't catch him. We walked a ways and got lost." He looked at the feeble fire, almost out "We were gettin' cold, so we built a fire. I had some matches in my coat."

Stillman heard footsteps and turned to see Jody walking up on the camp from the east, holding his Winchester across his body and frowning curiously. The youngest boy, Robert, whose blond hair poked through die holes of his cap, grinned delightedly. "Hi, Jody!"

"Robert? Edgar? What are you two doing out here?"

"We were huntin' and ole Thunder spooked at a magpie," little Robert said. "He bucked us off and took off, probably headed home."

"We started walkin' and somehow after an hour came to the place we started out from," Edgar added sheepishly.

"Yeah, that can happen out here," Jody said. "How did you get so far from home?"

Edgar scowled and looked at his hands clenched before him.

Robert said, "Edgar was followin' a big bull elk," he said, eyeing his older brother scornfully. "Wanted to shoot it and show it off to Prissy Schotz."

"I did not!" Edgar protested. "I just wanted the meat! He'd have dressed out huge and filled our whole smokehouse for a year!"

Young Robert chuffed and shook his head.

To Stillman, Jody said, "These are the Huard boys. They live with their mother and uncle in Blacky's Coulee, a good seven miles from here as the crow flies."

"Their mother must be pretty worried by now," Stillman said, eyeing the two boys. "Maybe she sent their uncle out after them."

"Uncle Ralph is off to Big Sandy," Edgar said. "He's gettin' lumber and wire for a new chicken house."

Shit, Stillman thought. He'd have to make sure these boys found their way home, and that could take precious time away from his tracking of Shambeau. He gave Jody a look that said as much, and Jody tightened his lips in complicity. It was a confounding situation, but there was nothing they could do about it until morning.

"I bet you boys are hungry," Stillman said.

Robert's eyes brightened. "I'll say we are!"

"Well, we'll set up camp, build up that fire, and see what kind of grub we can rustle up." Stillman started walking back for his horse. He turned back to the boys. "Oh, by the way, I'm Ben Stillman."

The boys looked at each other, their eyes growing large.

"The sheriff?" Edgar said, turning back to Stillman.

"Pleased to meet you," Stillman said, touching his hat brim, then walking off toward Sweets.

"Is he really the sheriff?" Robert asked Jody.

"He is at that, Rob," Jody said. "Didn't you see the star pinned to his coat?"

"I thought maybe he was just the deputy or somethin'," Edgar said.

"No, he's the real thing."

Edgar's eyes were large as saucers. "He's the one who shot Donovan Hobbs and solved that string of murders in the county last fall and sent that swine Norman Billingsley down to Deer Lodge?"

"One and the same," Jody said with a laugh. "You two sit tight. I'm gonna go fetch ole Dex."

The boys looked at each other and said in unison, "Wow!"

***

"There, that should keep you cozy," Stillman said later as he regarded the beds of pine boughs he'd made for both boys. "Now if we can get some food into you younguns, you can get some sleep and be ready to head for home first thing in the morning. I bet your ma's gonna be some happy to see you."

"You gonna take us, Sheriff?" Edgar asked.

He was sitting on a deadfall log, watching Jody tend the spit he'd erected over the fire and upon which two young rabbits roasted. Jody had brought the rabbits from home—two cottontails his nephews had shot earlier that morning. He was also tending a pan of corn cakes sizzling in the grease dribbling off the rabbits.

"I reckon Jody and me'll both see you home," Stillman said, trying not to sound too disgusted over the dilemma. "One of you can ride with me and one can ride with Jody."

"If we had one more horse, they could go on alone," Jody said thoughtfully. "I can give them decent enough directions."

"Well, we just have the two horses, so we'll take them," Stillman said. "Besides, I have a feeling ole Louis'll be holed up in that first cabin of his for quite some time, while that wound heals."

"Louis?" Robert asked. He was sitting on bis pine bough bed, his back against a log, holding a tin mug of coffee in his gloved hands.

"Louis Shambeau," Jody told him. "That's who we're after."

"We seen ole Louis," Edgar said. "About midday, just before our horse threw us."

Stillman and Jody looked at each other. Then Stillman turned to Edgar. "You saw Louis Shambeau?"

"Yeah, he crossed our trail and headed up a ridge. How

come you're trackin' him, Sheriff?"

Stillman ignored the question. "Where did this happen, son?" he asked, regarding Edgar intently. "Where did you see him?"

Edgar thought a moment, his eyes wide, and turned to look eastward along the stream. "Well, I thought it was back that way, but now I'm not sure. All I know, there was a big rock sticking up off a butte, and there were a lot of trees around it. There was a stream a little bigger than this one nearby, too." Edgar paused, thinking. "Oh, yeah, and we'd just passed an old tipi frame some Injun left in a clearing."

"I know the place, Ben," Jody said. "It's off one of the feeder canyons to Aspen Valley."

"How far away from here?"

"About an hour's ride."

"If he was there at midday, how far ahead of us would that make him?"

Jody shook his head and exhaled. "I'd say at least a half day, maybe more. And if he's traveling at night, like he probably is, we won't catch up to him till he's at his cabin. He probably knows a lot more trails in these mountains than the brush wolves."

"Well, at least we know we're heading in the right direction. I was worried he might have had another plan in mind, or another cabin you didn't know about."

Stillman turned to Edgar. "How did he look, son— could you tell?"

Edgar scrunched up his eyes and peeled his lips back from his big, square teeth, thinking hard. "Uh . . . seems to me he was kinda hunkered down in his coat. Yeah, I think he was, like he was extra cold or somethin'. It wasn't that cold then. The sun was out, and it was pretty warm for the mountains."

"He's hurtin', then," Jody said.

"Doesn't sound like the wound's slowin' him down any, though."

Jody flipped the corn cakes with a spatula. "I don't see how the man could have crawled up out of that ether as fast as he did. When those men who robbed the army paymaster shot me in the Hawley cabin last winter, it took me a good two days to sleep off the ether the doc gave me when he dug the bullet out."

"This man's different," Stillman said, tossing the coffee grounds from his cup and reaching for the pot. "He's not made of the same stuff as you and me. He's a survivor...at all costs. More animal than man, living by instinct, overcoming weakness by ignoring it and doing what he has to do to keep going... to keep living and breathing and eating."

"How come you're after ole Louis?" Robert asked, watching Stillman wide-eyed from across the sizzling fire. "Did he kill someone?"

Stillman regarded the boy seriously, the corners of his mouth curving grimly, the flames reflected in his deep-set eyes under the brim of his high-crowned Stetson. "Yes, he did, son."

Robert's voice was filled with urgency and awe. "How come?"

Stillman glanced at Jody, then returned his dark eyes to Robert. "Because they were bad to him. They pushed him

too far when what they should've done was left the man
alone. You don't bother men like Louis Shambeau. They're
tied to a different time, with different ways that might seem
odd to some, impossible to understand to others. But that
doesn't mean you don't respect them, treat them the way
you'd want to be treated, and give them a wide berth when
they want to be left alone."

Edgar cleared his throat, transfixed by Stillman's words.
"If they were bad to him, how come you're hunting him,
Sheriff?"

Stillman took a deep breath and flexed the muscles in
his neck. "Because he broke the law," he said, removing his
hat and running a hand through his shaggy salt-and-pepper
hair. He donned the hat again and smoothed his mustache.
"He broke the law."

Stillman sipped his coffee and stared into the flames.

They ate the rabbit and corn cakes, both boys so hungry
that they broke the bones and sucked the marrow out as
Stillman and Jody watched them and chuckled, shoveling
more food onto the lads' plates. When it was time for sleep.
Stillman chucked several good-sized branches on the fire so
they'd all stay warm. It was a clear night, with lots of stars
capping the pines, and the damp spring breeze had a penetrating chill.

Stillman slept hard, waking up occasionally to toss
more wood on the fire then falling swiftly back into a deep,
dreamless sleep.

At dawn he was jolted awake by the sound of approaching horses.

CHAPTER FOURTEEN

"JODY."

Stillman touched the young man's arm as he got swiftly to his feet, donned his hat, and grabbed his Henry.

Jody lifted his head as he tipped his plainsman back from his eyes. "What is it?"

"Riders."

Jody flung off his blankets and jumped to his feet, reaching for his gun belt and wrapping it around his waist. Stillman walked westward from the camp, holding the rifle in his arms and peering down the shadowy trail hugging the stream. Jody shouldered up beside him, listening and watching.

"I don't hear anything," young Harmon said.

"I could feel the vibration in the ground. Horses. A half dozen, maybe more, headed this way."

After a minute Jody said, "You sure? I don't—" He stopped as shadows moved upstream, separating from the boulders strewn down the side of. the mountain. "I'll be damned. Who do you suppose?"

"I reckon we're gonna find out in a minute," Stillman said, jacking a round into the Henry chamber and snugging the butt to his hip, just above his gun belt.

The riders grew out of the pale dawn light and stopped suddenly about a hundred yards away. They'd seen Stillman and Jody standing before them on the trail.

"What now?" Jody said.

"I don't know but be ready for anything."

The men milled around on the trail for several minutes, then came on slowly, two out front, six or so following in a straggly line. They were cantering now, backs stiff with apprehension, wondering, like Stillman, whom they'd run into.

When the riders were about thirty yards away, Stillman took several steps forward and planted his feet and held his rifle across his chest. "All right," he called. "That's far enough. Name yourselves."

There was a five-second silence. The men had halted on the trail, checking their horses down. One of the mounts whinnied. Another blew.

"You first," the leader called.

"Ah, hell," Stillman groaned, recognizing the voice.

"What is it?" Jody asked.

"Not *it* but *who.*" Stillman raised his voice and waved an angry arm. "Come on in, Hendricks. It's Stillman."

The leader gigged his horse ahead and the others followed suit. Hendricks approached on his big, black Morgan cross, a wry smile on his lips. "Gave me a bit of a spook back there, Stillman. But then, when I seen two of you, I figured you couldn't be Shambeau."

Stillman's features were angry, his voice tight. "What

the hell are you doing here? I thought I told you to keep your apes in their cages."

"That you did." Hendricks allowed. "But that was before you caught Shambeau, not *after* you let him get away."

"You tell him, boss," Tommy Falk grumbled. He was riding behind the rancher, sporting a red bandanna. His face was pinched and mean.

"Well, I'm telling you now," Stillman ordered, "get the hell out of here. Go back to your ranch and stay there, or I'll arrest you and all your men here for interfering with a lawman."

"You listen to me, Stillman," Hendricks said, jutting his head out over his saddle horn. "That madman killed two of my men and scalped another. You can't expect me to just sit back and listen to how you found him and let him get away. That renegade needs to be taught that if he messes with a Bar 7 man, he messes with all of them, and he pays the price."

"I'll arrest all of you, Hendricks," Stillman warned.

"No, you won't," the rancher defiantly retorted. "How could you? Besides, it would take too much time and you don't have much time before that mountain man gets so deep in the river breaks, he's gone for good."

Stillman stared levelly at the rancher, fuming. The man was right. If he and his men wanted to hunt Shambeau, there was little Stillman could do about it. He couldn't arrest them all out here. Even if they went passively, he'd be expending too much time.

Stillman raked his eyes across the nine horsemen glower-

ing at him and Jody, who stood beside him, cutting his eyes at
Stillman expectantly.

"All right," Stillman said at length, anger snaring his vocal chords. "I can't turn you back, but I sure as hell can tell
you how it's gonna work. You'll ride with me and Jody here,
and take our orders. The first one of you that gives us any
crap goes home, and I'll arrest you later."

Stillman glared at Hendricks. "I'm holding you personally
responsible for the conduct of your men. They get out of
line, you're out of line."

Hendricks scowled and narrowed his eyes. "No judge is
gonna—"

"There aren't any judges out here, Hendricks," Stillman
said, his eyes glinting with unadulterated rancor.

He let that sink in as the Bar 7 riders glanced around at
each other, incredulous, insolent expressions playing on their
craggy faces.

Regarding the two packhorses the men had brought
along for camping supplies, Stillman said, "First thing I'm
gonna do is appropriate one of your horses."

Hendricks cut another sharp look at him. "What?"

Stillman poked a thumb over his shoulder, where Edgar and Robert Huard watched the activities wary-eyed.
"Those boys back there need a horse to ride back to their
ranch on. One of your packhorses will do." Stillman
started moving toward the pack mounts at the back of the
group. "Someone give me a hand stripping the packs off
this dun."

Stillman stopped abruptly as the Bar 7 foreman, Dave

Groom, spurred his horse toward Stillman and leveled a rifle at him. "No one *appropriates* Bar Seven stock. You can talk a good game, Stillman, but you're just another tin star to me."

Stillman glanced from Groom to Hendricks, who stiffened in his saddle and bunched his mouth smugly.

"Oh—I must not have made myself clear," Stillman said affably, turning and giving his back to Groom.

He wheeled back around, grabbed the barrel of Groom's Winchester, and gave it a hard yank, twisting it free of the foreman's grip. Clutching at the rifle, Groom lost his balance and tumbled out of his saddle, hitting the ground on his ass.

Spewing epithets, the man was bolting to his feet when Stillman, holding the rifle by the barrel, jabbed the stock viciously between Groom's parted lips. Groom's head whipped back, and the foreman gave a painful cry, grabbing his mouth.

"Just to clarify," Stillman said casually, regarding the group, "anyone gives me any trouble, they get it back in the form of a smashed mug. Any questions?"

Groom was on his knees spitting blood. "You ... you broke my damn teeth!"

"You're lucky it was just your teeth, Dave. Next time I'm gonna ram the stock so far down your throat it'll take all your buddies to pull it out your ass." Stillman ejected the cartridges onto the ground, then tossed the rifle at the cursing, spitting Groom.

"Now," the sheriff said to Hendricks, "I want the packs off

that horse pronto!"

His face having flattened out and lost its color, Hendricks stared at Groom. Regarding the other men askance, he said grudgingly, "Phipps, Olnan—off with the packs."

Heading back to the camp, Stillman grumbled, "Now if everyone will just stay out of my hair, I'm gonna drink some damn coffee."

Edgar and Robert Huard stared at him awestruck as he passed. Jody locked eyes with the boys and smiled.

When Edgar and Robert were mounted on the back of the dun, Jody gave them directions back to their ranch one more time.

"You boys be careful now," Stillman said. "Keep an eye on the landmarks Jody told you to follow, and you should be home in an hour or so. Don't try any shortcuts."

"We won't, Sheriff Stillman," Edgar said.

Robert grinned. "Thanks, Sheriff. Thanks, Jody."

"Bye, boys," Jody said. "Tell your uncle Ralph I'll be over for afternoon coffee one of these days."

Stillman slapped the dun's rump and the horse cantered off, Robert turning around to wave and smile. When the boys had disappeared around a bend, Stillman and Jody turned to the Bar 7 men, who'd had coffee around Stillman's fire and were now tightening their saddle cinches, ready to ride.

Stillman sighed darkly, eyed Jody with a scowl, and headed for Sweets, all saddled and waiting under a pine.

"You can pick up your packhorse on your way back to the Bar 7," Stillman told Hendricks, who'd mounted his big Morgan.

"You're damn right I will," the rancher grouched.

Stillman untied his reins from the pine branch and mounted the bay. He turned to Dave Groom sitting his paint horse beside Hendricks. "How's your mouth, Dave?"

The foreman seemed to have gotten the blood stopped, but his lips were puffy and blue. When he sneered at Stillman, the sheriff could see that his two front teeth were gone.

Stillman said, "Well, Dave, instead of sending you back home, I'm gonna let you ride along as a reminder to the others to watch their p's and q's."

With that, Stillman tipped his hat at the flint-eyed foreman and gigged his horse eastward along the stream.

Jody sidled up to him on his buckskin. "Better be careful, Ben. You're liable to get another bullet in your back."

"Nah," Stillman said, kneeing Sweets into a canter. "They're kill-hungry, all right, but their anger's more for Shambeau than me."

"I sure hope you're right about that."

They rode for several miles, Stillman and Jody out front, Hendricks and his men behind. Few words were spoken.

It was a clear, bright day. Small birds sang in the pine branches, and raptors hunted along ridges. Once, a red-tailed hawk flew up from a great, dead birch, flapping its shaggy wings and screeching its way skyward.

Jody reined his buckskin to a halt in a narrow valley cut by a rushing stream. "There's the tipi poles the Huard boys were talking about," he said, pointing to an open horseshoe in the creek.

"Shambeau's trail must be close," Stillman said.

"What's that?" Hendricks asked, cupping an ear. He and his riders had reined up behind Stillman and Jody.

"We should have his sign soon," Stillman said crisply, reining his bay around to face the Bar 7 crew. "Now I want to make this clear, so I don't have to repeat myself again. I appreciate you boys helping me and Jody track Shambeau. It's right civic-minded of you. But if any of you interfere with the arrest, or try to take justice into your own hands, I'm going to nail you colder'n a grave-digger's ass. Understand?"

They just looked at him askance, squinting their eyes. Several were smoking.

"Understand?" Stillman barked.

"They understand!" Hendricks barked back.

"Good. Now, all of you stay the hell back so you don't foul the sign."

Jody had gone on ahead. Stopped in the trail about forty yards farther on, he called, "I've got it, Ben."

Stillman gigged his horse up to where Jody sat gazing at unshod hoof tracks.

"They cross the main trail here, arid head right up the mountain, looks like."

Stillman glanced back at the Bar 7 riders sheepishly appro, "hing. He sighed and told Jody to lead the way.

They rode up the mountain through a thick stand of aspens, then followed the curving peak for a quarter mile southward before turning back east and descending a game trail skirting a slide. Jody took the lead, leaning out from his saddle arid following the sign.

They cut elk and bobcat sign and ran across wolf scat by a spring runnel carved through a sandstone levee.

"This is griz country, Ben," Jody said fatefully.

"Let's just hope we don't see any."

"They'll probably stay out of our way, as long as we stay out of theirs."

Stillman urged Sweets down a crumbling slope. "Probably."

He was more worried about the Bar 7 riders than he was about bears. He wasn't worried about what they might try to do to him, but what they were bound and determined to do to Shambeau. It was his job to see that that didn't happen. It was his job to bring Shambeau back, unharmed if possible, to stand before a judge and jury.

On the other hand, why not just let them all go at it— the Bar 7 riders and Louis Shambeau? The mountain man had taken his revenge, so why not let die Bar 7 men take theirs?

It was a tempting thought, but an impossible option for one simple reason: It was against the law. Stillman's job was to uphold the law at all times and in all situations within his jurisdiction. If he allowed this backwoods, eye-for-an-eye justice to run its course, he'd be no better than the vigilantes he was trying to hold at bay.

Besides that, the sides were decidedly uneven.

At noon they stopped for lunch and to rest their exhausted horses. Stillman poured himself a cup of coffee, took note of Tommy Falk cleaning his Winchester under a tree and Dave Groom bathing his bruised lips with a damp rag, and walked out away from the fire.

He mounted a slight rise and surveyed a broad valley opening below. The cut was spotted with cedars and ash and flat-topped island buttes and was topped with a clear blue sky into which a few high, hazy clouds were beginning to slide in from the southwest.

Stillman was scanning the clouds, hoping they did not portend bad weather—a spring blizzard, say, which could be deadly in this country—when he heard grass rustling behind him. Turning, he watched Walt Hendricks approach with a cup of coffee, the collar of his bearskin coat pulled up against the chill breeze. He wore a fur hat and leather gloves. Fur mittens protruded from the pockets of his coat.

"I just want you to know, Stillman, I have nothing against you personally."

Stillman stifled a laugh. "That's good to hear."

"This is all just part of the game Louis Shambeau started himself."

"No, it's part of the game your men started, when they shot his mule."

Hendricks looks skeptical. "Huh?"

"The kid didn't tell you that part, eh?" Stillman nodded. "Falk shot his mule."

"Then he was probably trespassing on my land again—trapping my streams when I've warned him not to over and over again!"

"Shambeau doesn't understand the idea of 'your' streams any better than the full-bloods do. He was trapping them long before you came here and started calling them yours."

"He's a conniving thief—a cattle rustler. We've found the remains of more than a dozen cattle lying about my land."

"You have proof it was Louis?"

"Who else would leave nothing but the damn hooves and horns? The man is a renegade—a conniving, thieving murderer, and he has to be stopped. One way or another."

"That's what I'm out here for, Hendricks. If you and your boys would go home and leave me and Jody alone, we could get it done a hell of a lot easier."

"Uh-uh," Hendricks said, shaking his head and smiling knowingly. "Something tells me you're not so eager to catch this man, Stillman. Something tells me that if you're not watched, you're liable to let him get away. Why that is, I have no idea. Sentimentality, I guess. Some people just can't let the old days go, when men like Shambeau were a dime a dozen out here. Well, those days are gone, and men like Shambeau have to go. They're impeding progress. Having him running free in these mountains is like having a rogue grizzly on the prowl. Only ole Louis's not just killing cattle, he's killing men, too."

"Let's leave that up to a judge and jury."

"And why don't we leave his capture up to my men?" Hendricks's grin over the rim of his steaming cup was cunning. "A couple of 'em aren't half-bad trackers. They'll get him, might even bring him back alive, if possible. Meanwhile, you and I could be back at my ranch, talking over the old days over cognac in my study."

Stillman gazed at the man, expressionless.

"It would be our secret," Hendricks continued. "And it would mean a lot to my men. You've seen the looks in their eyes. Then we could all get back to work...."

Stillman smiled and shook his head. "We've yammered long enough, Hendricks." He tossed out his coffee and headed toward the fire and his horse.

"It would be worth a few dollars to me, Stillman—for you and me and Harmon to just ride out of here, leave my men to their work. More than a few dollars, as a matter of fact."

Stillman stopped and regarded the man dully. He was about to say something, then let it go. Shaking his head, he walked back to the fire.

It was nearly sunset when they stopped their horses in a deep, cedar-choked ravine filled with shadows and crusty snowdrifts. Jody and Stillman dismounted, and while the others waited, they took their rifles and walked down the ravine, avoiding rocks and pushing through pine boughs.

Jody hunkered down on his haunches and pointed into another ravine running perpendicular to this one.

"There it is," he said. "Shambeau's cabin."

CHAPTER FIFTEEN

EVELYN VINCENT BRUSHED her long, blond hair in the mirror over her dresser, working slowly but vigorously to bring out the shine. When she finished, she set the brush down and applied a little more rouge to her cheeks. From her admittedly dubious past experience, she knew that men like Bledin Carstairs preferred women with as much face paint as a Sioux warrior.

She smiled at the comparison, feeling only a little relief from her fluttering heart. The relief fled with the knock on her door, her heart beating again fervently.

"Yes?"

"Your gentleman caller's waiting downstairs, dear." It was Mrs. Berg, the widow who ran the rooming house in which Evelyn had lived since moving to Clantick nearly two years ago.

"Tell him I'll be right down, will you, Mrs. Berg?"

"Certainly, dear. Take your time."

Willing the nervous flush from her face, Evelyn peered at herself in the mirror, pulling here and tucking there on her yellow calico dress—the spring dress she'd sewn over the winter with material she'd bought with the money she'd earned hustling grub at Sam Wa's Café.

She pushed up a little on her bosom, rolling her eyes at herself and snickering, then carefully donned the dress's matching hat, pinning it to her hair. When she finished, she froze suddenly, arms hanging at her sides.

What she was about to do was not only crazy, but, if Carstairs was what she suspected—a professional robber— it could be dangerous, as well.

But the way Evelyn saw it, she had little choice. She'd overheard bits and pieces of Carstairs's conversation with the other two men in Sam Wa's cafe—hearing just enough to pique her curiosity as only the young, inquiring Evelyn's curiosity could be piqued. From what she'd heard, she gathered the men were up to no good. It sounded to her like they were about to pull some kind of robbery here in town.

Evelyn had once run with robbers herself. In fact, it had been a gang of train robbers that had brought her to Clantick before Ben Stillman, encouraging her to walk the straight and narrow, had gotten her the job at Sam Wa's. She knew how thieves' minds worked. Who better than she could infiltrate the trio and find out what they were up to?

She knew she should discuss what she'd overheard with Leon McMannigle. She'd almost done so but had stopped herself when she'd realized there was nothing he could do before the robbers took action—after money had been taken and, possibly, people had been killed. Also, Leon would only try to talk her out of her dangerous plan, and she didn't want to be discouraged. Foolhardy as it might appear on the surface, it was the right thing to do. Clantick was her town, its citizens her friends. They'd been kind to her when she'd needed it most. This would be her way of repaying them.

"Oh, who are you kidding?" she asked herself now. "You're enjoying this masquerade."

It was true. While for the most part she cherished her life here in Clantick, she had to admit it could get a little dull at times. Infiltrating the trio of robbers might be just the distraction she needed.

Still, she was nervous, and her hands were sweaty. Suppressing her misgivings, Evelyn took a deep breath and grabbed the white lace shawl from the back of the rocking chair. Arranging it across her shoulders, she said, "Well, this much excitement should tide you for about a year, Miss Vincent... if you live through it."

After a final glance in the mirror, she gave herself an encouraging smile, strode to the door, opened it, and stepped into the hall.

"Your gentleman is waiting, Evelyn," one of her sister boarders announced, snickering, as the girl passed on her way to her room. Over her shoulder, the girl added, "Cuts a right smart figure, too..."

Evelyn feigned a proud grin, inhaled again deeply, and headed downstairs. She passed through the front hall, and, thankful she didn't see the kind but persnickety Mrs. Berg, who would disapprove of all the makeup she was wearing, walked through the foyer and onto the front porch where Bledin Carstairs stood, facing the yard and smoking a stogie.

Hearing her footsteps, he turned and grinned, dressed to

the nines in a black cutaway suit, fawn pants, and boiled shirt. His black boots shone like silver, and a diamond pin pierced his wide, black cravat. Evelyn had known a lot of phony dandies in her time, but never one quite so phonily dandified as Bledin Carstairs, and she had to work hard at suppressing a snort and calling up an expression of girlish admiration.

Carstairs spoke first. "Ah, Miss Vincent, how ravishing you look!"

"Oh ... well, thank you... Mr. Carstairs," she said, filling her voice with humility and awe as she raked her eyes across his well-garnished frame. "But I don't look anything compared to you." Knowing instinctively that men like Carstairs preferred their women meek—the meeker the better—she meekly averted her eyes. "I'd like to say the dress is store-bought, but not on a cafe girl's salary. I made it last winter up in my room."

"You made that?" Carstairs said with overly animated surprise. "I never would've known."

Evelyn flushed again and looked around. "I thought for sure Mrs. Berg would be out here. She usually grills all the gentlemen callers for quite some time."

"Oh, I got the grilling. Yes, indeed," Carstairs said, puffing on the stogie, his gaze lingering on her bosom. He stepped forward and took Evelyn's hands in his, lifting his eyes to hers. "But it was a surprisingly short visit for a woman who so obviously keeps a very watchful eye over her boarders. She must have liked what she saw, eh?" Chuckling, he tendered a charming wink.

"You do cut a fancier figure than most of the callers we get around here, Mr. Carstairs." The strong smell of his cologne, which seemed to cover the entire porch, nearly pinched her windpipe shut, and she found herself inconspicuously gasping for air.

"Please, call me Blade."

"Only if you address me as Evelyn."

"Evelyn it is. And now I think we'd better start walking before you have me blushing like a schoolboy."

He offered his arm, and, taking it, Evelyn rolled her eyes. Meekly, with the air of a girl thoroughly intimidated by her suitor, she let him guide her down the steps of the wide stone veranda and through the gate in the wrought-iron fence surrounding the yard.

"I thought a walk along the river might be nice since it's such a lovely spring evening," Carstairs said. "Then maybe a quiet meal in the Boston?"

"Oh, the Boston!" Evelyn exclaimed. "Really? Oh, I couldn't—it's so expensive!"

"Oh, for heaven's sake, dear girl," Carstairs cooed, patting her hand which he held firmly in the crook of his arm. "That is not for you to worry about. You just leave the tawdry details up to Blade. All you have to do is enjoy yourself. You work hard—I've seen how you work!—but tonight you shall be served."

"Oh, my God!" Evelyn shrilled, her voice catching a little as she choked on a particularly potent whiff of his cologne. "Am I dreaming?"

Arm-in-arm, they walked along Third Avenue to First

Street, which they crossed, heading northward down the grassy bank to the Milk River curving between scattered box elders and aspens. Tiny, pale-green leaves were just now opening from the tight buds they'd been sporting for a week. The air was cool but fresh, and the river whispered in its chalky banks.

A perfect night and a perfect place for a lover's stroll, Evelyn thought with a wry pucker of her mouth. She hadn't dated many men since coming to Clantick; she'd had plenty of offers but few that had really interested her. She thought how ironic it was to be strolling along the river now with the very kind of man she'd been avoiding.

"So tell me, Mr. Carstairs," she said abruptly, trying to catch him off guard, "what kind of a salesman are you, anyway?"

He looked at her quickly, vaguely disconcerted. "What ... what do you mean?"

Feigning humor at his reaction, Evelyn laughed and tipped her head against his shoulder. "I mean, what do you sell?"

She felt his shoulders relax slightly, relieved. "Oh... what do I sell? Well... I sell farm equipment. We all do—the other two gentlemen you met in the cafe and myself."

"You mean, you bring farm equipment out here on the train?"

"No, no." Carstairs chuckled. "At least, not right away. We bring catalogs and brochures which we show to the farmers and ranchers we visit. When they decide on a purchase, we fill out order forms and return the forms to the company.

The orders are then processed and the machinery sent out, by train, in due time." He'd spoken precisely and automatically, like an actor reciting lines which he'd rehearsed.

Evelyn was feeling plucky, feeling the urge to toy with the arrogant man. "What kind of machinery?"

"What kind?" Glancing up, Evelyn noticed a flush wallow up from his freshly shaved cheeks.

"Yeah, you know—what kind of machinery do you sell to the farmers?"

"Well, all kinds, of course, Evelyn. Our company makes, uh, well over a hundred different types."

"Like ...?"

Carstairs chortled nervously. "Well, there are plows, of course, and hay rakes ... and ... there's the ole harrow." He placed his left hand on hers and squeezed it playfully. "What farmer could get along without the ole harrow, eh?"

Charmed, the simpleminded waitress giggled.

"And there is, of course, a vast array of other implements in our catalogs, and if I got started describing each, you'd never shut me up! No, no. Enough about me, my dear Evelyn. Tell me about yourself."

"Me?" Evelyn said as he helped her down a particularly steep spot in the trail along the river. She paused a moment, wondering what to tell him, then deciding that the truth about her past was probably just what the doctor ordered for this occasion. "Me? Well, I grew up in Iowa, and, well, I kind of didn't get along with my family too well, and I ran off when I was fifteen with a—oh, what will you think of me?"

"No, no—go on. With whom did you run off?"

"An outlaw." Evelyn gave a self-conscious laugh, flushing with chagrin.

Impressed, Carstairs turned to her with arched brows and humorous eyes. "An outlaw? Well!"

"Oh, he wasn't really an outlaw, but he wanted to be, and I thought he was at the time. Really, he was just a poor, bored farm boy who read too many of those illustrated newspapers and got the notion he wanted to be famous, like William Bonney or Black Bart. I went west with him to Colorado where he and another boy proceeded to rob trains. Well, they only robbed one—or half a one, I should say. They were both killed by the express agent. Cut in half by a shotgun. It was awful!"

"You saw it?"

"No. I was waiting for them in a nearby town, but I read about it in the newspaper a few days later, long after they should've returned." She did not have to feign the sadness in her voice.

She and Carstairs had stopped along the trail, and he watched her with thoughtful surprise. "My goodness, Evelyn—what an interesting tale."

"Yes, well, unfortunately, it's the truth. I don't tell everybody, you understand? What would people think? I've turned my life around now. I have a good job and am making an honest living. One day I might even get married to some nice man and have a whole passel of kids. Maybe raise some chickens and goats."

"Sounds very upstanding."

Evelyn giggled as if slightly amazed at herself. "It does, doesn't it?" Regaining her composure, she looked at Carstairs solemnly. "You don't think any less of me, do you—for the story I told? I was awfully young...."

"Oh, Evelyn, of course not," Carstairs assured her, patting her hand. "We've all done things we're ashamed of. And, like you said, you were young. No, no. Not at all!" He was smiling at her, taking quick darting glances, she noticed, at her breasts. What was it with men and breasts?

"Well, I've certainly turned my life around now," she continued, exaggerating her stiff upper lip. "I sometimes work ten- and eleven-hour days, if Sam needs me."

"It must be rewarding, but also very tiring   "

"Oh, it can be tiring, but I like it, Mr. Carstairs—Blade, I mean. Really, I do," she added, as though trying to convince herself as much as him.

"Are you hungry, Evelyn? Shall we head over to the Boston?"

Evelyn put a gloved hand to her mouth to cover a nervous titter. "Oh, gosh, the Boston!"

Carstairs had reserved a table in the back of the hotel's elegant dining room. When he and Evelyn were seated, he ordered a bottle of champagne and made a show of sampling the stuff before he allowed the waiter to fill first Evelyn's glass, then his own.

When the waiter had drifted away, Carstairs lifted his glass, his eyes unconsciously raking Evelyn's bosom again before climbing to meet her eyes, which she had to try her best not to roll. "To a beautiful young woman whom it was my good fortune to meet in the unlikeliest of places."

"Oh, gosh. Thank you, Blade," Evelyn said as demurely as she could, touching her glass to his and bringing the champagne to her lips with a thoughtful air.

"What is it, dear?" Carstairs asked her, concerned.

Evelyn shook her head slightly, ruffling her blond bangs about her forehead. "Oh, I was just thinking about what you said about the 'unlikeliest of places.' "

"Oh, certainly I didn't mean to denigrate—"

"Oh, of course you didn't. But it is an awfully remote place, isn't it? I mean, even here, in this elegant dining room which you were so kind and generous to bring me to, you can tell we're a long way off the beaten path...a long way from ... interesting things."

She sighed, gazing out the window at the street, virtually empty at this hour but for the occasional duo or trio of cowboys heading for a saloon. "A long way from excitement."

Carstairs gazed at her over his glass. "You miss excitement, do you, Evelyn?"

"I guess ... a little."

"Well, to tell you the truth—" He paused, set his glass down, and folded his beringed hands on the table. "May I speak frankly, Evelyn?"

"Certainly."

"I think it's a shame that such a lovely young damsel as yourself has holed herself up in this town. Nothing against Clantick, but it is a little far from the beaten path. It is, to be frank, a backwater. A woman like you, Evelyn, could certainly appreciate the finer things to be offered in places like Denver and New Orleans...."

Evelyn lowered her eyes to her plate and fiddled with a spoon. "I thank you for your compliments, Mr. Carstairs— you certainly know how to make a girl feel special—but how on earth could I ever get to places like Denver or New Orleans?"

"All you need is the right opportunity, my child," Carstairs said in his silky voice with his roguish grin. "Just the right opportunity." With that, he lifted his glass again and clinked it against hers. "To opportunities!"

Over dinner they talked some more about other things, and Evelyn knew he was feeling her out, making sure she was who she said she was and that her motives were genuine— that, indeed, she was with him solely because she found him charming and attractive, not to mention the most suave and interesting human being west of the Mississippi and north of the Equator.

For her part, it wasn't hard to convince him of that. He was guarded and cunning and certainly not whom he was pretending to be. Nevertheless, Carstairs, like most men, was a complete sucker for a girl's veneration. By the time their dessert arrived, Evelyn believed that with a few more demure drops of her eyes and one or two more of the exclamations with which she'd been punctuating his windy lies, she could have had him on his knees, begging for her hand in marriage.

She watched him covertly as he ate his cake and knew he

was mulling over an idea. Her heart thumped hopefully. Finally, he set his fork down, sipped his coffee, and wiped his mouth with his napkin. He looked at Evelyn resolutely.

"Evelyn?" he asked. "How badly do you want to get out of here?"

Feigning shock at the question, she shrugged her shoulders and fidgeted around in her chair. "Uh, I don't know, Blade. I..."

He glanced around the room. Seeing that the closest other diners were a safe distance away, he said in a low voice, "What if I told you I'm not really a salesman?"

He waited for this to sink in. Taking her cue, Evelyn frowned curiously. Her heart was increasing its beat, and her ears were beginning to ring.

"Well, if you're not..."

"I don't want to go into detail about what I am. What I can tell you is this: I can get you out of here, with quite a lot of money and more where it came from."

She stared at him bug-eyed.

"Sounds good, eh?" he said alluringly, slitted eyes flashing.

Slowly she nodded, keeping her eyes large. She was a simple, down-and-out girl with a shady past and her eye on a sudden rainbow.

"At noon tomorrow, I'll send an envelope with a stage ticket and travel money to your boardinghouse. We'll meet in a town to be disclosed later. You only have to do one thing."

She swallowed and cleared her throat. "Which is ..."

"Do you know the deputy—McMannigle?"

"Of course," she said tentatively.

"Go to his office or wherever he may be at four o'clock Thursday afternoon—four o'clock sharp—and distract him for about twenty minutes."

"Distract him? How?"

Carstairs dropped his eyes to her well-filled dress and smiled cunningly. "I'm sure, dear Evelyn, you can think of something."

CHAPTER SIXTEEN

STILLMAN WOKE THE next morning about an hour before dawn.

Lifting his head from his saddle, he looked around at the silhouetted figures of the Bar 7 men lying here and there around the dully glowing fire. Several were snoring. One smacked his lips and sighed, saying something unintelligible. Another lifted his hand and scratched his nose.

All were asleep, which was exactly what Stillman wanted.

Rising quietly, he slowly reached down for his gun belt, purposefully brought it up, and strapped it around his waist. Breathing quietly and keeping his movements to a minimum, he shrugged into his coat, donned his hat and gloves, picked up his rifle, and crept off down the ravine, watching his step as it was still too dark to make out the terrain.

"Jody, it's Ben," he whispered as he came to the point where the ravine abutted the one in which Shambeau's cabin lay.

He stopped and looked around, seeing only the silhouettes of trees and a few rocks. Gauzy clouds hung low, snuffing the stars. Something rustled to his right, and he turned to see a figure step out from the cedars upon the opposite bank.

"Here, Ben," Jody said, moving down the hill. "I found a better place to watch the cabin—on a rise above the trees."

"Any movement?" Stillman asked. He'd taken the first watch, Jody the second, while the Bar 7 riders snored. Fundamentally lazy, none had protested much about being excused from the night-watch rotation.

Stillman hoped the kid slept until he and Jody had Shambeau in hand. He hoped they all did. He didn't want the hammer-headed drovers interfering with his arrest.

"No movement," Jody said. "It was so still and quiet, I think I would have heard him if he'd left."

"Let's hope he's asleep. He rode hard yesterday with that shoulder." Stillman looked at Jody. "You ready?"

"Ready and rarin'," Jody said with an eager grin.

"Now, remember," Stillman cajoled, holding up a finger for emphasis. "You're stayin' outside while I bust into the cabin."

Jody sighed tolerantly. "You've told me, Ben, eight or nine times now."

"If there's any shootin' and ole Louis happens to be the one to walk out alive, you take him if you have an easy shot. Otherwise, turn around and run like hell."

"I know, I know—don't take any chances. Have I ever mentioned you sound like my old man?"

"Ain't no call to get nasty," Stillman said with a grin.

Turning, he headed into the abutting ravine, climbing across the uneven, water-cut terrain and pushing quietly through pine branches and bramble. At the bottom of the ravine, there was a stream just wide enough to make jumping it impossible. Not wanting to get his boots wet, for wet boots squeaked, Stillman found a rocky ford, and skipped across cleanly.

Young Harmon wasn't so fortunate. His left foot slipped off the last rock, soaking his boot to the ankle.

Stillman looked at him sourly. "You're better at trackin' than walkin'—I'll say that for you, kid."

"Sorry."

"Come on—*quietly.*"

They climbed the slope through the pines and cedars, Stillman slowing his pace so Jody could keep up without his soaked boot squeaking like a rusty wheel. The sheriff paused occasionally to get his bearings. It was hard to tell where the cabin was, for he couldn't see it in the darkness and from this deep in the ravine. He had to reckon by his memory of where he'd seen it last night before the light had died.

He paused behind the bole of a pine tree. When Jody had come up behind him, he pointed left and headed that way, his rifle in his right hand, breathing through his mouth, which was quieter than breathing through his nose. He also watched the ground for loose rocks and twigs he could kick or snap. A man of the mountains and forests, Shambeau probably slept as lightly as a sow grizzly with cubs.

Stillman paused, catching a whiff of pine smoke. It seemed to be floating down the side of the ravine to his right, where the bank sloped up through bushes and scattered rocks and chalky outcroppings. Heading that way about fifty yards, Stillman paused when he came to a small clearing and crouched behind a lightning-topped cottonwood.

He looked up the grade and saw the cabin humping darkly against a slab of granite topping the ravine wall. It was a small affair, with a lean-to shed off its right side and shrouded in pines and cedars. Smoke puffed from a chimney pipe and flattened out across the sod roof, tattering under a downdraft.

A woodpile sat to the left, offering cover close to the cabin. Before heading for it, Stillman wanted to know if Shambeau's horse was in the lean-to. One whinny from the horse could blow the whole thing.

Jody came up beside him, limping on the wet boot. "That's it, eh?"

"Yeah. Do you see a horse—?"

A sound cut him off. It had been the sound of a pebble rolling, and it had come from the cabin. Simultaneously, he and Jody crouched low, casting their glances toward the hovel and the rock slab pushing up behind.

"Did you hear it?" Stillman whispered.

"Yep."

They waited, staring. Shortly. Stillman saw a figure move atop the granite slab to the left of the cabin and about thirty feet above its chimney pipe. At first Stillman thought the figure was a hunting cat. Then it rose on two feet, and another figure appeared to its right. Both "cats" were carrying rifles.

Stillman was rock still. His voice was a tight rasp. "Son of a duck."

"Who is it?" Jody whispered.

Stillman watched the two men descend a narrow trough in the slab behind the cabin, rustling bushes as they did so. His stomach felt like lead and his chest ached with apprehension and anger.

As the figures stole around the right side of the cabin, moving from rear to Irani, keeping under the overhanging eave, Stillman saw that one was wearing something red atop his head—the same red as Tommy Falk's bandanna. Silently Stillman reprimanded himself. He should have checked to make sure all the riders were in the camp before he'd left. Instead, he'd been satisfied with a cursory glance and had obviously missed the absence of these two.

Why did he think the taller of the two was Dave Groom? Groom, being the foreman and having lost his two front teeth in the humbling midst of the men he supervised, probably felt he had a point to make—damn the lanky devil to hell and gone ...

A horse's whinny rose from the lean-to, and Stillman cursed.

"What do we do?" Jody whispered.

Stillman turned to reply, but before he could rake air across his vocal chords, a surprised yell followed by an agonized cry stopped him short. The first yell was followed closely by another, and by the time Stillman had whipped his gaze back to the cabin, the figures were gone.

At least, their bodies were gone. Their startled cries filled the night and pricked the hair along Stillman's backbone.

"What the...?" Stillman mumbled. "Did you see?" he asked Jody.

Young Harmon stared with a dazed, befuddled expression at the cabin. "No, I was lookin' at you."

Stillman was staring at the cabin, wondering what the hell had happened, what the hell was going on, when a blue-red light flashed in one of the windows, and a rifle barked. The slug tore into the fallen cottonwood he and Jody were crouching behind.

"Get down!" Stillman yelled as another light flashed in the window. It was followed by another rifle crack and another slug tearing bark and splinters from the cottonwood.

The trapper's horse whinnied and kicked the corral—a flitting shadow right of the cabin.

"Those stupid devils," Stillman rasped, lifting his head above the log and swinging the Henry around.

Jacking a shell, he fired. He jacked another round and fired again, hearing the slugs hitting the cabin with solid bangs. He brought the Henry back down and ducked behind the cottonwood as Shambeau fired back, three angry shots splitting the quiet night, one of the bullets spanging off a rock in the forest behind Stillman and Jody.

"You keep your head down," Stillman told Jody as he lifted his rifle.

"Come on, Ben. You can't take him alone. He's on to us now!"

"Keep your damn head down!"

"All right, all right."

Stillman shot twice and ducked as Shambeau returned his fire. So it went for the next several minutes, a useless exchange of lead, neither man hitting his mark.

Stillman thought he might be able to pink Shambeau through the chinking in the cabin logs, but the man must have applied the mud good and thick, probably to ward off the winter cold. There were two glassless windows, one on either side of the door, and the trapper moved between them effectively, further confounding Stillman's efforts at hitting his target.

"If they're not already dead, I'm gonna kill those two," Stillman groused, meaning Falk and Groom.

Something rustled in the woods behind him. Someone kicked a rock.

"Oh, crap," he said as he squeezed off a round at the cabin. He turned around.

"Stillman!" It was Hendricks.

The Bar 7 men must have heard the shooting and come running. Stillman could hear them snapping twigs and rasping orders in the forest around and behind him. He shook his head and spat another curse. All he needed now was a passel of trigger-happy brush poppers to really turn this into a Dodge City free-for-all.

"Walt, dammit—keep your men the hell back!"

But it was too late, and he knew it even before the men started shooting from various points around the cabin.

"Hold your fire!" Stillman shouted, but his voice was swallowed up by the thunderous clamor swarming up around him, the din of the repeaters spitting lead as fast as the waddies with their tails curled could jack the levers.

The din continued for about ten minutes. Stillman just sat there behind his log, shaking his head, Jody hunkered down behind him, hearing the thunder of the rifles and the thwacks of the bullets hitting the log walls. After the horse was killed, there were only two deviations in the sounds, and those were the surprised, angry cries of men whom Shambeau, firing from his virtual fortress, had found with bullets.

The cries evoked no sympathy in Stillman. He wished the trapper would send them all to the devil's doorstep. It would save him the trouble of arresting them, which he was by God going to do once he got back to Clantick. If any of them survived, that was.

This shooting was futile. Shambeau was well-protected behind those stout logs. Stillman was ready to settle back and wait for the Bar 7 men to run out of bullets when someone shouted, "Hey, look! Fire!"

Stillman peered over the cottonwood.

Sure enough, a wavering, umber glow shone in one of the windows, from far back in the cabin. Suddenly it flashed up, spreading.

A few seconds later Stillman felt the air sucked out of his lungs and, at the same time, a hot wind smacking his face, blowing his hat from his head and filling his eyes with grit. Close on the wind's heels came an explosion so loud it sounded like God applauding, shaking the trees and buckling the earth and blowing the roof off the cabin, grinding it into toothpicks borne on a ball of orange flames and flinging it beyond the treetops.

The shock wave picked Stillman about two feet off the ground and threw him back about ten yards. Feeling wood and cinders from the cabin raining upon him, he quickly turned onto his belly and covered his head with his arms. He lay there for what seemed a long time before the sound of the cabin roof thunking and thumping back to earth, snapping branches on the way down, finally ceased, leaving an eerie silence in its wake.

Slowly he lowered his arms and lifted his head, looking around

Bits of wood and brush from the cabin roof lay burning or smoldering on the ground and in the branches around him. He saw Jody lying six feet away. He was facedown and hatless, his coat covered with grit and ash and wood slivers. He peeled his hands from his face and lifted his head, looking around warily.

When his eyes met Stillman's, Ben said, "You all right?"

The kid glanced back along his body, making sure all his parts were there, and moved his legs. "I... reckon. What the hell happened?"

"Appears ole Louis was storing bang juice."

"Dynamite?"

"Probably used it for well-digging or stump moving or... who the hell knows?" Stillman sniffed the air. "Smell that? Magic Powder."

Stillman climbed tenderly to his feet, feeling creaky and bruised. His ears were still ringing, and his eyes felt sandblasted. He strode forward, stepping over the log he and Jody had been using for cover.

Regarding the cabin, he whistled softly through his teeth. There was little left but a pile of burning rubble. The front wall had been blown wide, away from the cliff behind the cabin, and spread across the clearing in small, burning snags. The side walls were half-standing but wouldn't be for long. The whole mess was ablaze, sending cinders floating on air currents. The clearing was lit up like a torch.

The air was thick with a fetid mishmash of burning pine, gunpowder, and skunk oil—the man must have stored gallons of the stuff—and burning animal hides. Chunks of wolf and marten furs lay a few feet to Stillman's left, smoldering and making his nostrils pucker.

Jody sidled up next to Stillman. "Well, I guess that takes care of ole Louis."

Ben nodded thoughtfully.

Before him, on the ground about six feet before the burning cabin, something moved. Instinctively Stillman crouched and grabbed the revolver from his holster, thumbing the hammer back.

"Don't shoot, damnit!"

It was Tommy Falk. He appeared to be climbing out of a rectangular hole before the cabin. His head bobbed, then his arms appeared, heaving his body out of the hole.

He got a leg up, dug a boot into the ground, and rolled

clear, coughing on the smoke and cinders filling the air around him.

Stillman and Jody ran forward, each grabbing an arm, and half-dragged, half-carried the kid to the edge of the clearing, where they dropped him unceremoniously against a tree.

Hendricks and one of his men, both sporting a layer of ash and dirt, were standing nearby and gazing awestruck at the blue-faced Falk, who was fighting what appeared to be a losing battle to regain his breath. He'd lost his bandanna in the conflagration, and his scabs were oozing blood and pus.

Stillman, Jody, Hendricks, and the Bar 7 rider watched as the kid slowly regained his wind and leaned back against the tree, lolling his head back and forth against the trunk.

"I swear that kid has nine lives," Hendricks chuffed.

"He's gonna wish he had ten by the time I'm done with him," Stillman said. He glanced back at the hole from which the kid had appeared, grumbling, "What the hell?"

"Bear trap," Jody said.

Squinting his eyes against the heat of the burning cabin, Stillman moved toward the hole, Jody, Hendricks, and several Bar 7 riders, who'd emerged from the woods, following suit. Shielding his face with his hat, Stillman gazed into the hole, grimacing at the grisly sight

A half-dozen stout branches, their ends whittled to spear points, jutted from the bottom of the hole. Draped over them, as though bent over to tie his shoe, was Dave Groom, several spears protruding from his back. His arms and legs hung at his sides.

Stillman shook his head as he stared at the bear trap into which Groom and Falk had fallen. The kid must have avoided serious injury by lighting along an edge of the hole, where there were no spears.

"The trapper must have had it covered lightly with wood and dirt, and the kid and ole Dave didn't see it," Hendricks speculated.

"What in the hell did he have a trap this close to his cabin for?" one of the riders snapped, grimacing down at the hole.

"With all the butchering and skinning he did in there," Jody offered, "he probably had all kinds of unwanted visitors prowling up to his door. Not the least of which was probably bears."

"Yeah, I'd have me a trap out here," another rider said, looking warily around the remote clearing, which was paling now as the sun rose. "Too bad ole Dave had to fall into it, though."

"Well," Hendricks said, turning away from the hole, "at least he won't have to worry about his smile anymore."

Stillman gazed at the cabin with a look both pensive and relieved. "That's the end of ole Louis, I guess," he said with a sigh, donning his hat and starting away.

"I don't think so, Ben," Jody said, grabbing Stillman's arm. "Take a look."

Stillman turned and peered down Jody's pointing arm into the cabin, where the fire was beginning to run out of fuel. Through the thick, wafting smoke, he saw the cabin's back wall, which was the face of the granite cliff jutting up behind it. In the cliff was a crack just wide enough for a man to walk through sideways.

Stillman scowled at Jody. "You telling me there's a back door to this place?"

Jody didn't say anything. He and Stillman looked at each other. Then, cursing under his breath, Stillman wheeled and ran around the side of the cabin to the cliff face behind it.

CHAPTER SEVENTEEN

STILLMAN CLIMBED THE trough in the granite cliff, sending rocks and pebbles rolling down behind him. Breathing hard, he made the crest.

The sun was an opal smudge on the eastern horizon, and the sky had paled considerably, offering a wider field of vision. To Stillman's right, aspen branches with curled, dried leaves lay strewn about the pitted granite slab in a straggly line. They had to have been placed there, for no aspens grew within a hundred yards of the place.

Pulling the branches aside, Stillman uncovered a crack in the granite running back from the cabin for about fifty feet. A yard wide in places, the fissure traversed the entire width of the granite slab, opening onto a deep valley filled with rocks and pines.

Stillman's heart pounded. Sure enough, this was the back door to Shambeau's cabin, which the trapper had no doubt used before the dynamite had been ignited by the fire.

Stillman muttered an incoherent string of curses as he removed the last of the branches and stepped into the fissure, walking toward the corridor narrowing so much at times that he had to turn sideways. There was a slight elbow he had to sidestep around, and then, before him, at the end of the fissure, he could see the back of the smoldering cabin.

Glimpsing something at his feet, he squatted down and picked up a piece of relatively fresh bannock. Shambeau had no doubt dropped it from a packsack on his way through the passageway, on his way toward freedom. Tossing it away, Stillman gave another exasperated curse, turned, and headed back out the way he had come.

When he emerged from the rock, Jody, Hendricks, and several Bar 7 riders were waiting for him looking incredulous.

"You mean to tell me that son of a duck got away?" Hendricks barked.

Stillman looked at Hendricks, who stood with the morning wind buffeting the fur in his hat, his expression turning tentative and sheepish, his eyes lurking within the puffy foxholes of their lids. He knew Stillman was furious and didn't want to say anything more to fuel his fury. For Stillman's part, he wanted to pummel the rancher with his fists, but knew that doing so, while making him feel better, would be a foolish waste of time and energy.

The man had been supposed to keep a tight rein on his men and hadn't, but nothing Stillman could do now was going to change a damn thing. His biggest mistake had been letting the Bar 7 crew ride along, but if they hadn't ridden along, they would have tried tracking Shambeau themselves and really fouled everything up.

Ignoring Hendricks, Stillman turned to inspect the ground where the corridor opened onto a gentle grade falling away to another valley. He picked up several mocassin prints and followed them until they disappeared in a large bed of shale carpeting about fifty square yards among stunted pines and junipers.

"Hoofing it in those moccasins, he's not going to be as easy to track as he would on horseback," Jody said, scouring the ground as he made his way slowly across the talus.

The Bar 7 riders watched him and Stillman from the granite ridgetop.

"That's no doubt his plan," Stillman said grimly. At the edge of the talus, he slowed and pointed. "Here we go," he said. "I've got him again."

Bent over, scrutinizing the faint trail through the blond brush, he followed the prints through cedars, over a knoll, around a boulder, and down the mountainside. Jody caught up with him at the bottom of the valley, near a spring bubbling around an uprooted Cottonwood.

"They head that way down the valley," Stillman said, pointing southeastward.

"Slippery devil."

"How much of a lead you think he has on us?"

Jody squatted to scrutinize the tracks. "I'd say half an hour. He's probably a mile beyond us."

Stillman glanced at the sky splashed with low, charcoal clouds. "Well, we'd better get our gear and get a move on before that snow hits."

Breathing hard, he and Jody climbed the ridgetop, then descended into the opposite valley, where the cabin smoldered in the clearing. Two of Hendricks's men had been assigned the gruesome task of removing Dave Groom from the hole while Falk and two others dug graves.

Hendricks was smoking a cheroot on a deadfall log, one boot crossed on a knee. "How many men you lose, Walt?" Stillman asked him, his level tone belying his anger.

"Two dead, with Groom. Another man got his ear damn near shot off, but he can ride."

"Good for him," Stillman said. He turned to retrieve his rifle.

"You pick up his trail?" Hendricks asked.

Stillman did not reply.

"Hey, Stillman," Hendricks called. "I...uh... I want to apologize for my men... for the kid and Groom. The stupid devils were working on their own when they stormed up to the cabin earlier."

Hendricks waited, but Stillman didn't say anything.

"It won't happen again," Hendricks assured the sheriff with an air of chagrin, studying his cigar ash.

Clutching the Henry, Stillman started down the hillside toward the camp. "No, it won't."

Frowning, Hendricks watched Stillman and Jody walk away down the hill. "Hey, where you goin'?" he called angrily.

Stillman didn't reply.

When they got back to the camp, Stillman and Jody quickly rigged out their horses, forgoing breakfast. The weather did not look good, and Stillman wanted Shambeau in hand before a possible storm hit. While tracking would be easier in the snow, an April squall could hold them up for days.

Stillman slid his rifle in its sheath and walked his horse to a tree. Tying Sweets to a branch, he said to Jody, "Hold your buckskin good and tight, son."

"What are you gonna do?"

Jody watched Stillman untie the rope picketing the Bar 7 horses between two pines. When the horses were free, Stillman unholstered his Colt and fired three shots over their heads, sending the bucking, kicking herd galloping away through the brush.

Stillman watched the horses disappear, feeling the ground rumble under their pounding hooves, and turned to Jody, who was grinning. "Well, that should keep the Bar Seven boys busy till, say, noon or so?" Stillman's mustache curled wryly.

Jody chuckled. "At least."

Mounting his horse, Stillman turned to see Hendricks and several of his men running red-faced into the camp, their eyes on the fallen picket line and the gap between the two trees where their horses should have been.

"Damn you, Stillman!" Hendricks raged.

Calmly Stillman kneed his horse over to the man, halting when his stirrup lay six inches from the rancher's protruding belly. "Now, it's gonna take you at least half the day to round up your horses, Hendricks. When you do, go home. The first man I see out here again—you, Falk, or any of the others—is gonna get a bullet courtesy of the sixteen-shooter riding my saddle boot."

"That's against the law!"

"That's my word," Stillman said. "Good as bond."

He heeled his horse forward into the main ravine, and started down the hill, letting Sweets pick his route to the bottom.

***

He and Jody picked up Shambeau's trail a half hour later, after skirting the granite cap, and followed it along the valley bottom for nearly an hour before it suddenly climbed a saddle. From the saddle, it descended a shallow ravine, cut back northward through a snaking gorge, and appeared again on a wide, grassy plateau that had seen a fire in recent years. The pines and box elders stood darkly skeletal against a low, gauzy sky, the lightly falling snow limning their branches from which the bark had been seared.

Crows cawed and squirrels scuttled through the knee-high brush.

"It's funny, you know, Ben," Jody said as they rode along through the trees, keeping an eye skinned on the tracks. "He doesn't seem to be heading anywhere."

"What do you mean?"

"His sign. It don't seem to be following any definite course."

Stillman nodded. "He doesn't seem all that hard to track, either."

"What do you think it means?"

Stillman shrugged. "He's either just trying to run our asses off, hope we play out and have to turn back, or..."

Jody looked at him. "Or what?"

"He's playing with us. Leading us into an ambush." Stillman turned to Jody. "Keep your eyes peeled. Don't let your guard down."

Later, they lost the trail in a tangle of cedars and junipers. When they found it again, their horses were exhausted. Stillman found a good place to hole up for an hour, at the base of a towering rock. He built a fire and fried potatoes, which they ate with some of the rabbit Jody had brought along.

When they and the horses were rested and fed, they resumed the search for Shambeau, following his evenly spaced tracks through ravines, along a briskly flowing stream cutting through the badlands toward the Missouri River, which lay about ten miles south, and out along a grassy plateau. It was a frustrating endeavor, for even on level ground, where they could ride faster than Shambeau could walk, they never seemed able to close the distance between them and the trapper.

They stopped for the day about an hour before sunset, in a dry creek bed enclosed on three sides by a high bank and pine woods. The snow was still coming down, no harder or slower than before, but it had gotten colder. Stillman figured the temperature was hovering around ten or fifteen above.

They built a fire, brewed coffee, and fried potatoes and

the last of the rabbit

"You think the Bar Seven men went home?" Jody asked, buttoning his fly as he returned from the bushes.

Stillman poked the rabbit around in the skillet, the aromatic smoke wafting against his face. "If they know what's good for them, they did, but I wouldn't lay money on it. Hendricks is an old Indian fighter from way back."

Jody hunkered down across the fire, regarding Stillman with humor. "Would you really shoot him?"

Stillman looked at the young man pointedly. "After all the headaches him and his men have given me?" He grinned without humor and touched a finger to his forehead. "Right between that jasper's little eyes."

When they'd eaten, Jody rolled into his blankets and Stillman took the first watch. He sat several yards out in the creek bed, away from the fire so he could keep his eyes well-trained on the darkness that fell over them like a cold, black glove.

The snow stopped, but the clouds remained, blocking the stars. In the distance, off toward the Missouri, wolves howled. They were soon joined by several coyotes and, later, by a hunting lion. Closer by, raccoons laughed in the woods.

The sheriff smoked and thought about Shambeau for a while, then about Fay, missing her keenly as he always did when they were apart.

He'd gotten out his makings sack and was about to roll a cigarette when a shrill scream cut the silent night jolting him so violently that he lost half his tobacco.

***

Ten minutes before Stillman had heard the scream, Bernie Phipps was perched on the hillside above the Bar 7 camp, manning the first night watch with his rifle in his arms.

Phipps hunkered down in his deerhide coat, his hat pulled low over his ears, and stared down at the campfire around which the other Bar 7 riders slept in blankets, heads on their saddlebags and saddles. They were all snoring loudly, but none louder than Hendricks himself.

To keep his mind off how cold and miserable he was, Phipps thought about how Dave Groom's demise, tragic as it had been, left a gaping hole in the foreman's job at the Bar 7. That hole would need to be filled as soon as Phipps and the others returned to the ranch, and who better or more qualified to fill it than Bernie Phipps himself?

If you were talking seniority, Phipps was next in line for the job, for he'd hired on at the Bar 7 only two months after Groom had. All the other riders—all that were still alive, that was—had come later.

Not only did Phipps have seniority, but next to the kid he was the best damn bronc buster on the roll. He was a hard worker and a straight shooter to boot. Unlike Groom, he'd never taken one of the Hendricks girls out to the bam.

Phipps grinned naughtily. The pitch he would give to his boss faded as he remembered how he'd caught Groom literally with his pants down, pumping away between Miss Megan's naked knees, her blouse bunched around her waist, her squealing like a—

What was that?

His thoughts kicking back to the moment, his wet-lipped smile vanishing, Phipps jerked around with a grunt. Something had rustled the bushes behind him. Because he'd been staring at the fire, he couldn't see clearly, but he thought he saw a branch move back in the woods.

There was a slight crackling sound, like soft-soled shoes on pine needles.

Phipps jumped, bringing his rifle up and frowning, blinking the red streaks from his eyes. Adrenaline shot through his veins and a chill jetted up his backbone. He cocked his head, listening.

Again came the sound, softer this time, of crackling pine needles.

Phipps glanced down the hill toward the other men sleeping around the fire. He considered calling them, but what if this turned out to be a raccoon or a porcupine or, hell, just his imagination? He'd look like a fool. Knowing the belligerent cuss ole Hendricks could be, it might even hurt his chances of securing the foreman's job.

He turned back to the darkness, gripped his rifle in both hands, and started forward, moving slowly, one step at a time, ears pricked and listening.

When he'd walked up the hill about twenty yards, ducking under pine and fir branches, he stopped.

About twenty feet ahead, a shadow slipped out from behind the black column of a tree trunk, then disappeared behind another about six feet to its right.

"Hey, who's that?" Phipps growled, keeping his voice low. "Shambeau... that you?"

He started forward again, aiming the rifle at the tree. When the tree was only ten feet away, Phipps stopped, took a deep breath, and sprang forward around the pine, the stock of his rifle snugged against his cheek.

Nothing, no one, was there.

"Well, I'll be god—"

Another shadow flitted through the trees ahead, disappearing up the hill. Phipps stared, scowling, pondering, wondering if it was Milt Polly or Condor pulling a prank. He wished he would have taken a closer look at the group around the fire, so he'd know if one or two of the boys had been missing from their hotrolls.

"Okay, you son of a duck," Phipps growled, walking forward, making his slow, cautious way up the hill.

The farther he walked, the harder and raspier his breathing grew. When he finally made the brow of the hill, he was puffing and mentally cursing his last cigarette.

Muffled footfalls sounded dead ahead, down the other side of the hill. Vowing to shoot whomever it was, whether it was the loco trapper or one of his own, Phipps started forward.

He'd taken two steps before something clutched his left foot, grabbing him around the ankle. He was going down with a yell when he heard a snap.

And then suddenly his left foot was yanked out from beneath him.

And then, just as suddenly, there was a great whooshing

sound, and he was upside down and hanging from a rope tied to a tree branch. He lost his hat and heard the smack of his rifle hitting the ground beneath him.

"Ohhhh... *God!*" he bellowed in exasperated shock, completely dumbfounded, his mind a blur, watching the ground slide back and forth and feeling as though his hip were being wrenched from its socket, as though his blood were about to burst through his eyes and out the top of his head.

"Oh, Jesus... God... what the ... what the *hell?*"

Then something moved in front of him. It was a silhouette only slightly darker than the sky behind it.

The figure of a man took shape. Phipps stared at it, feeling his guts flood with bile, a coppery taste filling his mouth. His heart was in his throat, mumping across his vocal chords, rendering him mute.

Bernie Phipps couldn't see the man's face, but he knew it was the trapper. The man wore a wolf-hide coat and a fur hat, and a pack was strapped to his back. He carried what looked like an Indian's bow in his right hand and what appeared to be an arrow in his left.

The man moved toward Phipps and stopped about ten feet away. Methodically he brought the arrow to the bow, notched it, and drew it back against the string, the bow making leathery creaking noises as it tensed.

Phipps licked his lips and found his voice and cried, "Oh ... no ... you son of a ...!"

He heard the snap the bow made as it released the arrow. He heard the whistle of the arrow slicing air. And, squeezing his eyes shut, he heard the thump of the arrow tearing into his thigh.

That's when he screamed.

CHAPTER EIGHTEEN

JODY LIFTED HIS head from his saddle with a start. "What the hell was that?"

Stillman stood peering into the darkness, his Henry rifle in his hands. "A scream."

He walked slowly forward and stopped about twenty feet from the fire. Jody walked up beside him, clutching his revolver in his right hand, his hair mussed from sleep.

"One of the Bar Seven men?"

"Could be," Stillman said. "Whoever it was was in a hell of a lot of pain."

"How far away?"

"About a half mile, I'd say."

Jody looked at Stillman. "Think they found Shambeau?"

Stillman had opened his mouth to speak when another cry sounded, shrill with anger and anguish. The two horses nickered and fiddle-footed in the brush on the other side of the fire.

Jody started forward. Stillman grabbed his coat, holding him back.

"Hold on. Where do you think you're going?"

"Ben ..."

"There's nothing we can do. It could be a trap. Even if it isn't, the country's too rugged for night travel. We'll check it out in the morning."

They stood listening for several minutes. Stillman put his hand on Jody's shoulder. "You'd best get back to sleep. I'll wake you in a while."

Jody turned and walked back to the fire. He threw another log on the flames, then rolled up in his blankets.

Stillman stood in the darkness for several more minutes, wondering who was dying out there, and who was doing the killing. Deep down, he knew...

He'd returned to the fire and was pouring a cup of coffee when another cry lifted on the quiet night, causing him to slosh coffee over his cup rim.

Jody gave a start, lifting his head. "Jesus Christ! How long is he gonna scream like that?"

Stillman sighed and said grimly, "Till he's dead, I reckon."

"Isn't there anything we can do, Ben?"

Slowly Stillman shook his head. "By the time we got there—if we got there—it would all be over."

Jody pondered this, then cursed and threw his blankets back. "Think I'll have some coffee."

He sat with his back against his saddle, sipping his coffee and staring gloomily off in the darkness. Stillman did likewise, perched on a rock, his Henry standing between his knees. The night was utterly quiet, like a held breath.

No wolves or coyotes howled, and nothing scuttled in the brush. Stillman had never known a night so haunted.

When he finished his coffee, he rolled a cigarette. He no longer wanted one, but the screams had agitated him, made him feel nervous and eager for morning when he could find out what in the hell was happening. He needed something to do with his hands.

He'd just lit the cigarette when another cry rose, less fervent than the last. Trying to ignore it, Stillman smoked his quirley down to a nub. He squashed the stub under his boot as the man who was being tortured moaned.

It was a single, hopeless, utterly despondent bay, and it quickened Stillman's blood even more than the screams had.

Jody didn't say anything. He sat with his cup in his hands, staring and listening, his eyes wide and troubled.

After a while Stillman said with a fateful sigh, "Well, that should be the end of it."

"I wonder why none of the others helped him," Jody said solemnly.

Stillman stood and turned to the lad. "You gonna be awake for a while?"

"I couldn't sleep after that."

"Well, then, I reckon I will." Stillman set his Henry against a log and headed for his bedroll. "I have a feeling tomorrow's gonna be another long one."

He lay on one of his blankets and drew up the other, but it was a long time before he finally slept. He relieved Jody two hours later, and when Jody had slept restlessly for another hour, they saddled their horses and, as the sky began to pale, headed southwest along the creek.

Neither said anything. The night had shot their nerves.

When they came to a spur ravine, they followed it westward through a canyon and up a cedar-spotted hill. Hearing a horse nicker to his right, Stillman touched the butt of his revolver and turned.

About fifty yards below, Walt Hendricks squatted by a smoky fire in which a black percolator sat. The rancher held a coffee cup in his gloved hands. His black Morgan was tethered to a nearby tree, shaking its head at Stillman and Jody, and giving another nicker.

When their own horses nickered back, Hendricks looked up sharply and dropped his cup. He climbed heavily to his feet, clawing at the revolver holstered under his coat. He froze when he saw who his visitors were and gave up the awkward hunt for his gun.

Scowling, he hunkered back down on his haunches and poured himself another cup of joe, which he sipped as Stillman and Jody approached.

"Shoot me if you're gonna shoot me and get it over with," Hendricks snarled, staring into his fire. "I didn't go home, and I don't intend to go home until the trapper's dead."

Stillman brought his horse to a halt and studied the frenetic-looking rancher, who seemed much older than the last time he'd seen him. But just as stubborn.

"Where are your men, Walt?"

"Out beating the brush for Shambeau. He paid us a visit last night."

"I heard," Stillman said with a nod. "Who'd he get?"

"Phipps."

"Where?"

Hendricks gestured with his thumb. "Up the hill yonder. They haven't cut him down yet. I wanted you to see Shambeau's handiwork for yourself." He glanced at Stillman, his eyes dark with disdain. "Murderin' damn half-breed," Hendricks grumbled, cutting his eyes at Jody, then bringing his cup to his lips.

A half-breed himself, Jody stared at the man from atop his buckskin. His brown eyes were hard, his face expressionless. His left jaw dimpled at the joint.

Stillman turned to him, said, "Come on," and started toward the hill.

Jody sat his horse, staring at Hendricks.

Stillman halted his bay and hiked around in his saddle. "Come on."

Finally, Jody turned his eyes from Hendricks and spurred his horse after Stillman, and they rode through a scattering of pines toward the hilltop.

They were about forty yards from the crest when Stillman halted his horse suddenly, staring straight ahead. Jody sidled up to him, following his gaze, and said, "Is that what I think it is?"

"I'm afraid so." Stillman gigged his horse into a lope up the hill and stopped before the body hanging spread-eagle and upside down from a long Cottonwood branch.

Phipps turned gently in the breeze, the rope and branch creaking with the strain. The man's eyes were open and staring, his open mouth making a dark O. The terror was still in the drawn muscles of his face.

Arrows jutted from both thighs, both shoulders, and the dead center of his chest.

Stillman heard the thud of hooves and turned to see Hendricks riding up the hill on his big Morgan. The rancher had halted his horse and sat gazing up at the gently turning body of Bernie Phipps.

"We all wanted to help him, but I ordered the boys to remain in the camp. I had a feeling it was a trap. That maniac was using Phipps's screams to lure us onto this open hill, where he could gun us all down like ducks on a pond."

"No doubt," Stillman said. "Where are your men?"

Hendricks pointed south, where the Missouri River breaks spread out like a devil's maze of canyons and mesas under a chill opal sky. "That way."

Stillman lifted the collar of his buckskin mackinaw, said, "Let's go," and headed out, leaving the body of Phipps twisting and turning in the breeze.

"Why'd he do that, Ben?" Jody asked as they rode, Hendricks following. "Why did he kill Phipps like that?"

"What choice does he have?" Stillman said. "He's cornered, with nowhere to run. His only option is to turn and fight."

"So he's stalking us, now—is that what you're saying?"

"That's what I'm saying."

✶✶✶

Dave "Condor" Ulrich walked his zebra dun along a limestone escarpment studded with cedars and small pines and blew into his hands to warm them. He didn't like wearing gloves when he might have to grab his gun and shoot. He'd heard of more than one cowboy shot to death because he'd been wearing gloves in cold country, and his hand had slipped off the gun he'd been trying to draw.

Condor Ulrich, so named because of his hawk nose, close-set, penny-colored eyes, and head that had been pinched in his mother's birth canal and had never regained its natural shape, knew he could very well need his gun at any moment. What had happened to Bernie Phipps last night was all the warning he needed.

Shambeau could appear anytime, anywhere, and any man unprepared, as Bemie Phipps had obviously been, was going to die.

Letting his horse steer itself along the meandering game trail, Condor shoved his left hand into the pocket of the coat he'd sewn himself from cured marten hides, the fur of which resisted frost, and returned his right to the butt of his Colt revolver. He peered up at the sky, where high, soft clouds had parted, allowing several shafts of washed-out sunlight to angle down upon the patchwork quilt of water-scored terrain surrounding him.

Glancing over his shoulder, he saw the tawny-green Two-Bear Mountains jutting from the rising northern prairie, slashed with troughs and ravines and spotted with still-barren aspen woods. He wanted to head back into those mountains, cross ole MacGregor Ridge, take the Sunnybrook trail around Devil's Coulee, and head back to the ranch.

He'd had enough of hunting Shambeau. He wouldn't admit it to anyone else, least of all the hombres he rode with, but he was scared stiff of the crazy mountain man. He had a feeling nothing good at all was going to come of this. Nothing good at all...

Condor had stood against his share of men, bad hombres in some of the worst saloons and brothels north of the Mason-Dixon line, but he'd never run into anyone as savage and slippery as this half-breed trapper. He wished Hendricks would take Stillman's advice and call it quits, but there was little chance of that happening. Hendricks and the other men were fueling each other's fire, and any man suggesting they give up would be branded a coward forevermore.

They wouldn't go home until they had Shambeau's head on the end of a stick. And no one was going to keep them from accomplishing their objective, including Stillman.

Condor glanced around and frowned at something lying several feet away, near several large rocks and a talus patch. Curious, he dismounted, walked over, and kicked at what appeared to be a porcupine hide turned inside-out, the meat and bones gone. Looking around, he saw the bones, which looked like rabbit or coon bones, only stouter, strewn about the talus.

Condor hunkered down on his haunches and pondered the hide. He knew a grizzly would do this—roll a porcupine onto its back and scoop out its meat and innards through its belly, the only place on the hide which didn't sprout quills. But a grizzly would eat the bones as well and leave tracks. Looking around, Condor found no tracks. At least, not grizzly tracks. What he did find were the soft, barely noticeable indentations left by mocassins.

An Indian had been here, caught a porcupine, and eaten it raw. Or a half-breed who hadn't wanted to give his position away with a fire...

A chill started up from Condor's feet and lifted goose bumps on his back. He glanced around cautiously, then returned his gaze to the bones. They were dry, as was the blood, which meant the trapper had passed through here at least an hour ago.

Which meant he was probably a good ways from here by now.

Taking heart from the thought, Condor led his horse back along the trail he'd been following, and on which he now discovered occasional mocassin prints, or half-prints with a stitch or two showing here and there. Condor was wary; a warning pulsed within him, tightening his muscles till they ached. He did not want to follow the trail, but what else could he do—turn tail and run?

He scrunched his face miserably. Why did he have to be the one to have picked up the man's trail?

Reluctantly he followed the trail around a low escarpment and started onto a ledge jutting over a canyon. He'd had enough of this. He had a feeling he was getting too close. Just too damn close …

As he was about to mount his horse and ride away—to hell with the others—he saw a figure move out from a high rock ahead of him. Condor froze, his saddle horn in one hand, the cantle in the other. It was the worst possible position to get caught in.

His heart rolled over several times and his mouth went dry. Shambeau stood to the right of the rock, facing Condor with no expression on his face. His rifle was snugged up to his cheek, the octagonal barrel yawning wide at Condor's face.

Dave was frozen there, unable to move, every nerve in his body screaming with fright.

"Hey, Condor!" someone yelled from the canyon opening on his left. 'That you?"

A single hopeful note squirmed its way into the cataclysmic symphony thundering and clattering through Condor's ears. He turned his head slightly to his left, peering into the canyon. A man sat his horse there, about fifty yards away. It was the kid. Tommy Falk, his red bandanna orange in the faded sunlight.

Condor slid his eyes back to Shambeau. Falk couldn't see him because of the rock standing between them. The rifle remained snugged up to the trapper's cheek, the barrel yawning wide at Condor, not moving a hair.

Shambeau's eyes communicated instructions to Condor, who understood almost without knowing it.

"Y-yeah, it's me, Tommy."

"What in the hell you doing up there?" The kid's voice was brash, urgent, impatient.

Condor glanced again at the two dark eyes of the trapper, boring down on him along the stock of the Sharp's rifle in his hands.

"I... I... I was stoppin' to take a whizzer."

"Well, get a move on, damnit! You ain't doin' any good just standby there talkin' to your horse."

Condor smiled rigidly, his mouth drawn back in a line across his face. He wanted to say something that would make Falk stay, but he knew that as soon as he did, he would die. But he was going to die, anyway.

Or... maybe not. What was he reading in Shambeau's eyes? Was the man going to let him live, after all? Was he going to let him go?

Condor's heart thumped lightly, and a hopeful spurt of adrenaline warmed his brain.

"Yeah, I'm headin' out now," he called to Falk. He'd lowered his hands to his sides and was facing the trapper with that sick smile on his face.

"See that you do, damnit! Remember, we're all meetin' up again in an hour, back where we started."

With that, Falk turned away and spurred his horse forward. Sliding his gaze back and forth between him and the trapper, Condor watched Falk ride eastward around shrubs and low outcroppings along the canyon floor.

Meanwhile, Shambeau held the rifle steady on Condor's face—at a point, Dave believed, between his eyes and just above the bridge of his nose.

When Falk disappeared around a shaley dike, Condor turned to the trapper. Hopeful, he grinned.

The gun exploded, flashing, the fifty-caliber slug hitting the trapper's target with a thunk and a splash.

CHAPTER NINETEEN

FAY STILLMAN WALKED out the frosted glass doors of the Boston Hotel and stepped onto the wide white veranda. Behind her scuttled the hotel's dapper little manager, Henry Wade. He held the doors with more effort than necessary and smiled with the painful self-consciousness characteristic of most men who found themselves in the celestial presence of the sheriff's lovely wife.

"I think this arrangement will work out well for both you and Mrs. Wheatly," Fay said as she clamped her simple brown reticule under one arm and donned her kid leather gloves.

"I couldn't agree more, Mrs. Stillman. I know that anyone you recommend for employment at the Boston will be a most beneficial addition to my staff." Wade shook Fay's extended hand and gave a little bow, his florid face even more florid than usual. "I can expect her to report for work in one month, then?"

"One month it is, Mr. Wade. She'd be available sooner, but Marie wants to make sure Crystal will be able to manage alone with the baby. It's Crystal's first, you know."

"I completely understand. I'll be watching for Mrs. Wheatly, Mrs. Stillman. Please give her my regards when you see her again."

Fay glanced at the bright, cloudless sky. "I think that'll be today. It looks like a nice day for a ride." She smiled her burnished smile, which had been wrenching male hearts in northern Montana since she and Ben had moved to Clantick, then turned and descended the steps to the boardwalk. Turning right, she headed west along First Street, oblivious to Wade's lusty gaze on her backside.

Still holding one of the doors open, Wade heard a snicker. Turning, he saw one of the hired girls scraping bird dung off a windowsill with a putty knife. He knew the girl had seen him ogling Mrs. Stillman.

Flushing, he muttered curtly, "Be careful you don't scrape the paint, Patty," and headed back inside, the heavy door swinging closed behind him.

As Fay strolled westward along First Street, greeting people she passed, she felt good about securing the housekeeping job for Crystal's sister, Marie. But mostly Fay was thinking about Ben, as she had been doing for the past several days now since he'd headed into the mountains after Shambeau. As she stopped on the corner of Second Avenue for a trash wagon to pass, she hoped against hope she would find him at the jailhouse.

She knew she would not, however. If Ben had returned, she would have known about it by now.

But then again, he might have thought she was in school, as she normally would be on a weekday, and had decided to wait until noon to look for her....

As she approached the jailhouse, she slowed when she saw Leon heading diagonally across the street, pushing a handcuffed prisoner ahead of him. The man was much shorter than Leon, middle-aged, and dressed like a cowboy—a drover who spent very little of his monthly wages on clothes or baths. What he did spend it on was obvious by his heavy alcohol stench, which grew heavier as he and Leon approached the boardwalk.

"Mornin', Fay," Leon said.

"Good morning, Leon. I see you're, uh … indisposed." She produced a wry smile.

The drover reached up with his handcuffed wrists and grabbed the rumpled hat from his head. Bleary-eyed, he formed a snaggletoothed grin. "Mornin', ma'am. You sure are a sight for these sore old eyes."

Fay smiled at the man as though deeply charmed.

"Don't mind him, Fay," Leon said. "It was payday yesterday at the Running W, and every payday Roy Luther comes to town to turn his wolf loose."

"I don't mean no harm, ma'am," Roy Luther told Fay with a beseeching expression on his face. "I get to drinkin' and I just can't help myself...."

"We all have our vices, Roy Luther," Fay said reassuringly. She lifted her gaze to Leon. "I won't keep you. I just thought I'd stop and see—"

"He's not back yet," Leon said, obviously troubled. "I sure am sorry. If I hadn't—"

"Leon, please. It wasn't your fault."

"Well, of course it was my fault! If I hadn't let the doc talk me into drinkin' with him, Shambeau would be keep-in' house with ole Roy Luther right now."

The cowboy gained a fearful, wide-eyed expression. "I don't wanna be jailed with the likes o' that savage! Why, crossin' that killer's as dangerous as walkin' in quicksand over hell!"

Leon glanced at Fay. "Shut your mouth, Roy Luther!"

The cowboy looked sheepishly at Fay. "Oh ... sorry, Mrs. Stillman. I'm sure your husband, uh... I'm sure your husband can handle him."

"Come on, Roy Luther," Leon said, jerking the man toward the jailhouse. "Ben'll get him, Fay. You can bet on it. And I'll be sure and let you know just as soon as he and Jody hit town."

"Thanks, Leon," Fay said, turning away, not feeling heartened by the deputy's reassurances.

Stiff and lethargic with worry, she wasn't sure what to do now. She didn't want to go home and listen to all that silence. She could go over to the school and grade some papers, but then she remembered her idea to ride out to the Harmon ranch, to visit Crystal and inform Marie that Henry Wade had agreed to employ her at the Boston.

Glancing at her timepiece, Fay saw that it was nearly noon. She'd better have lunch before leaving town. With that thought in mind, she headed over to Sam Wa's Cafe where she hoped she'd find someone she could talk to while she ate and who could keep her distracted from her worries over Ben.

She was in luck. As she let the cafe door swing shut behind her, she saw Katherine Kemmett wave at the back of the room, which was already beginning to bustle with the noon dinner crowd. Katherine sat across from Doc Evans, who glanced over his shoulder at Fay sheepishly.

"Doctor, Katherine," Fay greeted as she approached the table. "Mind if I join you?"

"Of course you may, Mrs. Stillman," Katherine said. Glancing at the doctor with a look of scorching rebuke, she said, "If you don't mind the company I've been keeping of late. Shall I send him away?"

His eyes on his plate, the doctor wrinkled his nose.

"No, he can stay," Fay said, giving Evans a look of mock disapproval as she sat down. "I'm fairly incorruptible."

It was nice, having lunch with Mrs. Kemmett and the doctor. They talked about school and church and about the job Fay had landed for Marie Wheatly. They talked about the weather and how lovely the river looked this time of year and how nice it was to see and hear the Canada geese heading north again.

The conversation ended swiftly, however, when one of the Hemphill boys came in to inform the doctor and Mrs. Kemmett that his father had been kicked by their mule and was "seeing two of everything." After the doctor and Katherine had hurried away, Fay finished her sandwich and soup then gathered her reticule and gloves and headed for the counter to pay her bill.

"Thanks, Sam. See you soon," she said when she'd paid the proprietor.

She was heading for the door as Evelyn Vincent sprang

out of the kitchen with two steaming platters in her hands.

"Good-bye, Mrs. Stillman. I hope the sheriff gets back to town soon."

"I do, too, Evelyn. When he does, we'll have you over for supper again."

"I'd like—" Evelyn stopped, her eyes sliding to the door opening behind Fay.

Fay turned. Three men entered—strangers, all. They were all dressed in suits, derby hats, and boots polished to high shines.

"Well, hello there, Miss Evelyn," the first man said grandly, lifting his hat. He was the best looking of the three, but there was something about him—his cunning eyes, foxlike grin, and superior posture—that put Fay off immediately.

Evelyn greeted the men a little stiffly, her cheeks flushing, her eyes darting self-consciously between them and Fay.

"And hello to you too, ma'am," the first man said to Fay, lifting his hat and grinning down at her with his azure eyes flashing. She didn't approve of the way the man looked at her, his gaze quickly traveling the length of her body, measuring her with a subtly lascivious gleam in his eyes.

Fay gave a cursory greeting, unable to pretend she liked the man, and turned back to Evelyn, who still held the platters in her hands, smiling woodenly. "We'll see you soon, I hope, Evelyn."

"See you soon, Mrs. Stillman."

When Fay had stepped onto the boardwalk, she glanced back through the window and saw Evelyn talking to the leader of the three men, smiling and laughing nervously before excusing herself to serve the platters.

Fay turned away, knowing something wasn't right but uncertain what it was. She hoped the young waitress wasn't falling for the dapper gent with the wolfish grin. He had trouble written all over him.

Knowing it wasn't any of her business, Fay sighed fatefully and headed home where she quickly changed into her green riding habit and black felt hat, then saddled her black mare, Dorothy, in the stable connected to the chicken coop.

Shortly, she was riding south of town, the Two-Bears looming before her on their straw-colored pedestal of prairie, brushed with bright spring sunshine. The two places Fay felt most at home were in Ben's arms and riding out here on her frisky mare, and since she couldn't at the moment have the former, she set herself to fully appreciating the latter.

She galloped along benches, climbed knolls from where she sat and gazed across the foothills, and rested in hollows where Dorothy drank from the cool, rushing streams. Fay admired the season's first wildflowers, crocuses, showing their lilac-blue petals amidst the sage and blue stem, and smiled at the several large flocks of Canada geese splashing and barking in sloughs still flooded with the water left from the deep winter snows.

Red-winged blackbirds set the prairie alive with their ratchety nesting cries, nearly drowning out the more melodic notes of the meadowlarks. The air smelled earthy and fresh and wild.

"Hello, Mrs. Stillman," one of the Wheatly boys called as Fay galloped Dorothy through the main gate of the Harmon ranch.

"Good morning, Albert. Are your mother and Aunt Crystal home?"

"Yes, ma'am."

"Wonderful." Fay reined up at the corral, and the boy followed her over from where he'd been loading salt blocks into a short-bedded work wagon harnessed to two mules. "I see ranch chores are keeping you busy, Albert."

"Yes, ma'am. Especially with Uncle Jody gone. I hope he's back by next week, though. That's when calving's due to start."

"*Oh,* I'm sure he will," Fay said, giving voice to her own wishful thinking.

The fair-haired Albert, who was twelve, took Dorothy's reins. "Want me to grain her and give her a rubdown for ye, Mrs. Stillman?"

"Would it be too much trouble?"

Albert grinned, flushing. "Not at all, ma'am."

"Much obliged, kind sir."

Breathing heavily from the ride and throwing her hair out from the collar of her wool riding vest, she headed for the two-story cabin with its wide stoop upon which two cane-bottom chairs and a large washtub sat. Smoke poured from the stone chimney, no doubt keeping the cabin warm for the baby, whom Fay could hear crying inside.

The door opened as Fay approached the stoop. It was Marie Wheatly, Crystal's older sister, looking as shy and demure as usual. Fay assumed the woman's perpetually cowed demeanor was the result of her having been abused for years by her drunken, temperamental husband, who had burned their ranch buildings and disappeared after Crystal had urged Marie and the children away from the place.

"Hello, Mrs. Stillman," Marie said in her soft, sing-songy voice. It was a pretty voice but seemed always to be lacking in vigor. "What a nice surprise."

"Hello, Marie. How are you?"

"I'm just fine. Would you like to come in?"

"I would at that," Fay said, approaching the door which Marie held open. Entering the cabin, she removed her hat and turned to see Crystal standing and holding her crying baby before the enormous fieldstone hearth in the living room.

"You came just in the nick of time," Crystal said as she bounced the child in her arms, caressing his cheek with hers. "I was just about to throw this little varmint down the privy."

"Crystal!" Marie chided as loudly as Fay had ever heard the woman raise her voice.

"Oh, I'm just jokin', Marie," Crystal said, walking toward Fay and extending the baby in her arms. "Here— you wanna cuddle the little demon?"

"I'd love to take him!"

"Sucker." Crystal snorted. Mockingly, she said to her sister, "These women without children are the biggest suckers for a crying baby I've ever seen. I bet in a few minutes we'll have her changing his diaper, too, Marie."

"I would be honored to change his diaper," Fay cooed, grinning broadly at the blanketed bundle in her arms, the little pink face mottled from crying. "And how are you, my dear sweet William Ben?"

The baby's cry was high-pitched and loud, fairly rattling the windows.

"That about says it all," Crystal said as she headed into the kitchen. "He slept only about two hours last night, and he's been awake all morning. If you still want him by the time you leave, he's yours." Crystal turned to Fay with the brittle, exaggerated smile of a sleep-deprived young mother who had, somehow, retained her sense of humor. "Coffee?"

"Sure," Fay said with a laugh. "Pour me a cup." She cuddled the baby, rocking it gently, and gradually the child stopped crying and stared at Fay with its large, cobalt-blue eyes as though mesmerized. A few minutes later the round eyes grew heavy, and the child fell asleep against Fay's shoulder.

"Look at that, Crystal," Marie said as she set cookies on a plate, noting the quiet baby in Fay's arms. "He's settled right down."

"Just like his grandfather," Crystal quipped. "A sucker for a pretty face."

When Crystal had put the baby to bed, she returned to the kitchen where Fay and Marie had taken seats at the round pine table covered with a blue-checked oilcloth. "I take it there's been no sign of our weaker halves, eh?" Crystal asked Fay.

"Nothing yet," Fay said with a sigh. "I'm sure they're fine, though."

"Yeah, me, too," Crystal said, taking a seat across the table. "Ben promised to bring Jody back unharmed. He's never lied to me before...." But the dark light in her eyes as she brought her cup to her lips told Fay that Crystal had been as worried as Fay had been. "When I first saw you ride up," Crystal continued, "I got worried you had bad news, it being a school day and all. But then I saw you smiling at Robert."

"I canceled class for the day," Fay said. "Frankly, my nerves have been frayed a bit, and I felt like taking a day off." Brushing cookie crumbs from her lips, she turned to Marie. "Also, I have good news for you, Marie. Mr. Wade has agreed to hire you at the Boston."

Marie looked stunned. "Me?"

Fay reached out and clutched the timid woman's hand. "Of course you. You wanted me to inquire, didn't you?"

"Well... yes, but I never... I didn't think he'd actually consider *me!*"

"Well, he did consider you, Marie. Not only that, but you're hired. He's expecting you in exactly one month. Do you think you'll be ready?"

Marie blinked her eyes and set her coffee down carefully so she wouldn't spill it. Her face was flushed. "I-I don't know. Where will me and the children ... where will we live ... ?"

"That's been taken care of, too. Mrs. Merrivale would love for you to live with her until you can find a place to rent. You remember Dott Merrivale, don't you? She lost her husband a couple months ago, and her children are all grown. She has a big house all to herself, and she really took to the idea of having you and the children help her fill it. I talked to her after church last Sunday."

"My gosh, I..."

"You wanted to get on your feet, Marie," Crystal said. "Not that Jody and I don't love having you here. I mean, as far as we're concerned, you can live with us indefinitely. We have plenty of room, and we love the kids. But I know how important it is for you and the children to have a place of your own."

Marie took her cup in her delicate hands and sipped her coffee thoughtfully. Setting the cup back down, she looked at Fay. Fay thought it might have been the first time the woman had ever looked her in the eye. "Thank you so much, Fay. I'd like to... I'd like to give it a try."

Fay squeezed her hand, kissed her cheek, and smiled. "It's settled then. And you and Ben and I will be neighbors. Mrs. Merrivale lives just down French Street from us."

Fay stayed another hour, chatting with the women. When she was ready to leave, she went into the bedroom and kissed little William Ben good-bye.

"I think you need one of those," Crystal said as Fay returned to the kitchen.

"What's that?"

"A baby."

Fay thought about it, as she had thought about it so often in the past. She and Ben had discussed it, but he'd been reluctant because of his job and his age.

"You know what?" Fay said wistfully, longing again for her husband, wondering where he was and what he was doing... when he would return and when she would feel his big arms around her once again. "I think you're right."

CHAPTER TWENTY

THE BOOM ECHOED in the cloudy distance rimmed with grassy buttes and pine-studded rimrocks.

Stillman reined his horse to a halt. He glanced at Jody.

"What the hell was that?" Hendricks said, riding behind them.

Neither Stillman nor Jody said anything. They heeled their horses into gallops, gravel fanning out behind them. When they'd ridden a half mile along a sagey bench between two canyons, Stillman led the way into a hollow, through a swale bordered by rocky escarpments, and onto the bench on the other side.

About fifty yards away he saw a man standing by two horses on a finger of land jutting into another shallow canyon speckled with junipers and cedars. He heeled his horse that way and reined up as the man watched, one hand on the hogleg jutting up from a soft leather holster positioned for the cross-draw. The man wore a black, weather-tattered sombrero and a somber expression on his round, unshaven face.

On the ground behind him lay another man on his

back, the top of his head blown onto the talus gravel above him. His arms were outstretched, as though he were waiting for angels slow to appear.

"That damn trapper kilt Condor," the man said, glancing at the body on the ground. "The kid, Falk, he was talkin' to him just a minute before it happened—from down in the canyon there. The trapper must've had ole Condor dead to rights, and he was afraid to say anything, Dave was."

"Where are the others, Aver?" Jody said.

"They went off to track him. I stayed behind to bury Condor." The stocky cowboy, Aver Wilkinson, glanced at the body again sadly. "We bunked together, me and Condor." His jaw tightened and his eyes slitted, his face mottling. "When we catch that damned Shambeau..."

"Looks to me like he's catching us." Stillman said as he dismounted and handed his reins to Jody.

Hendricks rode up with his new Colt rifle in his hands, shifting his eyes from the cowboy to Condor Ulrich and back again. "What the hell happened now?" he barked.

While Wilkinson went through it again, Stillman crouched to inspect the body. There wasn't much to see but blood and brains, so he turned away. Seeing the porcupine carcass, he walked over and poked at it with his boot. He picked up a bone and inspected it closely.

"What do you have, Ben?" Jody said, dismounting his buckskin.

"Same thing Condor had before he bought the farm. Shambeau's last meal."

"Porcupine?"

"Sure. You've never had porcupine?"

"Unfortunately, it was one of Pa's specialties. But not even he ate it raw."

"He would have if he'd been on the hoof with men after him, not wanting to signal his presence with a fire." Stillman tossed the bone into some shrubs and looked around.

Hendricks had dismounted. Approaching Stillman red-faced and with his rifle in his arms, he said, "What the hell is going on here, Sheriff? Who's hunting who?"

"I think that's fairly obvious."

"You have a job to do, damnit! Why in the hell aren't you doing it?"

Before Stillman could answer, Jody said with a humorous air, "Uh, Ben, I'm gonna lead our horses into the canyon for water. There's a spring down there."

Stillman didn't reply. He was staring at Hendricks with no shortage of disdain in his gray-blue eyes. The rancher stared back through the two fleshy pockets in his face, the round top of his pitted nose turning pink. He swallowed and took one step back as Stillman moved toward him stiffly, hands straight down at his sides.

Out of the corner of his eye, Stillman saw something move to his left. Before he could react, a big-caliber rifle exploded with a deafening roar. Hendricks gave a start and a jerk, his face going slack. Blood shot from his right temple, splattering Stillman's coat.

As the rancher dropped to his knees, Stillman wheeled left, clawing iron. Shambeau turned and disappeared down an escarpment about twenty yards away.

The wide-eyed Wilkinson looked after the trapper in shock. "That *son of a duck!*"

Stillman crouched and raised his gun, but Shambeau was gone.

"Stay with Hendricks!" he yelled to the cowboy and took off running, climbing the escarpment in five fluid leaps. At the top he saw Shambeau clad in a wolf-hide tunic running westward along another escarpment. Stillman dropped to a knee and squeezed off two quick shots, both bullets spanging off rocks with high-pitched whines.

Bolting to his feet, Stillman ran, hurdling rocks and dodging boulders and low-growing pines. The escarpment jutted sharply to the left. Shambeau followed it, running hard, his rifle in his right hand, a packsack flopping against his back.

Stillman brought his gun up, took hasty aim, and fired twice more. Both shots sailed wide. Shambeau disappeared behind several boulders piled by a long-ago glacier.

Stillman cursed and ran, his boots crunching gravel and clattering on exposed shale and limestone slabs. He pumped his arms, his heart swelling with his eagerness to catch the trapper once and for all.

Suddenly Shambeau appeared ahead of him. The man was looking around him, hesitating, his heavy brows furrowed as though perplexed. He glanced back at Stillman approaching at a run, extending his revolver and thumbing back the hammer.

Stillman fired, but it was too late. Shambeau had

jumped off a ledge. Stillman ran to the ledge and peered over the cliff into a deep gorge cut eons ago by the river, hollowing it from chalky rock. Below stood a tall, straight pine, its top about thirty feet beneath the ledge.

Stillman's blood quickened when he saw Shambeau clinging to the trunk of the pine, a few feet from the top. The tree was wavering, slowly bowing with the trapper's weight.

Stillman hesitated, not quite believing what he was seeing. Then the tree bowed in earnest, the bark cracking, its top curving groundward.

Stillman aimed and fired his last two shots, both slugs snapping branches. Then he lowered his gun and watched Shambeau drop from a branch, hit the ground on his feet, stumble once, and run. He ran, limping slightly, until he disappeared around a butte. He was still carrying his rifle.

Stillman holstered his gun and stared at the tree, which had resumed its natural position. He bent at the waist, held his arms out from his sides, encouraging himself to do what the trapper had done. He could do it, by God, if Shambeau could.

Well, he who hesitates...

"Ben!" Jody called behind him.

It was too late. Stillman had jumped, free-falling from the cliff. He hit the pine with a violent thump, the air hammered out of his lungs, feeling as though his brisket had been split with a wedge. Pine needles and cones jabbed his face, poked at his eyes.

He felt the tree shudder and bow. Then there was a

loud cracking sound, and Stillman's heart fell as did the rest of him, plummeting through branches. He landed hard, feeling the pricks and pokes of the tree branches collapsing around him. The trunk spanked the ground with a roar and a rush of cool wind.

Stillman lifted his head, but everything was a blur. His brain pounded painfully.

He sighed. Everything went dark and quiet.

He woke later to Jody squatting before him and asking, "How many fingers am I holding up, Ben? How many fingers?"

Blinking groggily, feeling as though his skull had been split with an ax, Stillman looked around. The tree he'd brought down was nowhere to be seen. They were in a narrow canyon with a spring freshet running nearby. The horses were hobbled on the grassy bank. It was a tidy little place, and Stillman could see why Jody had picked such a bivouac. It had high walls and appeared accessible from only one direction.

The clouds had lifted, and the sun felt nice on Stillman's face.

"How many fingers am I holding up, Ben?" Jody repeated, an air of desperation in his voice. "How many fingers?"

Stillman pushed himself into a sitting position with his hands, grunting and groaning with the effort. "Three."

Jody sighed with relief. "How do you feel?"

"Old. How long have we been here?"

"A little over an hour."

"How in the hell did you get me here, anyway?"

"You walked, with my help. You said a few words—don't you remember?"

Stillman shook his head tenderly.

"Rattled your brains a little. Jesus, you never should've tried that jump."

"Now you tell me," Stillman growled. "Any sign of Shambeau?"

"No. I tried tracking him, but all the Bar Seven riders came running when they heard the shots. They got after him and muddled his trail. There's no way in hell we can track him now, with all those yahoos running through these canyons."

"Hendricks?"

"Wilkinson buried him next to Condor."

"Shit," Stillman growled.

"Yep. They should've taken your advice and gone home."

"How many of 'em are left?" Stillman was probing his temples with his fingers, assessing the damage. Jody had wrapped a bandage around bis head, over several wounds pitting his forehead. His face burned with shallow gashes, which Jody had apparently cleaned with the whiskey bottle and rag sitting nearby.

"Four. Falk, Wilkinson, Donny Olnan, and Milt Polly."

Stillman chuffed a mirthless laugh and dug his makings pouch from his shirt pocket "Well, we'll see how long they remain four. Here, roll me a smoke, will you, son? I don't think my fingers are up to taking instructions from my brain just yet."

"Sure," Jody said, going to work on the cigarette. "Then I'll build you a fire. Now that you're awake, I'll see if there's any trails the Bar Seven men haven't soured."

"Forget that I want you to go on home now."

Young Harmon's face blanched with disbelief. "What?"

"I appreciate your coming along with me, boy, and helping me track. But the tracking's over. Hell, Shambeau's trackin' us!"

"Ben, I'm—"

"Don't argue with me. I'm not taking any chances on you getting hurt. I promised Crystal I'd send you back to her and your son in one piece, and I aim to keep my promise."

"Forget it, Ben."

The lad's harsh retort dumbfounded Stillman. "What's that?"

"You heard me. You can just wipe the notion right out of your mind. I'm not leavin' this job until it's done."

"Now, wait—"

"No, you wait," Jody said pointedly, his jaw hard, his eyes resolute. "You aren't sendin' me home like some stall-fed tenderfoot. I'm stayin' here with you, and I'm gonna see this thing through to the end, and that's final." Jody crouched on his heels, returning Stillman's stare. He didn't so much as blink.

Angry, but knowing there was nothing he could do short of knocking the kid out, tying him over his horse, and spanking the buckskin home, Stillman gave a weary sigh and brought his cigarette to his lips, drawing deeply.

As he exhaled, he grumbled, "You sure have your old man's ornery streak—I'll say that for you."

"Thank you," Jody said with a grin. "Now I'll start gathering brush for that fire."

As he started off, Stillman called after him, his tone surly, "Stay close. Shambeau could be anywhere. Keep your eyes peeled and your gun handy."

Jody turned, frowning. "What are we gonna do if we don't track him?"

"Wait."

"Huh?"

"We're gonna wait right here. He'll either come to us or his shooting will lead us to him."

Jody gathered the brush and branches and built a small fire while Stillman dozed, trying to clear out the cobwebs. The hours passed slowly. Jody drank coffee and played solitaire. Later, he gathered some twine from his saddle-bags, fashioned a snare, and disappeared, reappearing an hour later with a fat rabbit, which he roasted on sticks over the fire.

***

It was nearly five o'clock, and he and Stillman were eating hungrily when they heard several soft clicks coming from the mouth of the canyon. Stillman dropped his supper, raked his gun from his holster, and swung toward the noise.

He chuckled and depressed the hammer as the deer, a white-tailed doe, turned quickly and bolted back down the canyon, its hooves clattering on the rocks and gravel.

"Damn near gave me a heart stroke," Jody said, setting his Winchester back down beside him.

They'd just begun eating again when they heard a shot.

Both men reached for their guns and froze. The rifle report had come from at least a half mile away. They looked cautiously around for several seconds.

"What do you suppose?" Jody said, tentative.

Stillman waited, listening. Then softly: "I don't know. He might've gotten one of the Bar Seven, or they might've gotten him. But let's sit tight. I have a feeling there's going to be more shots where that one came from."

He was right. About a half hour before sunset, all hell broke loose in the direction of the river.

CHAPTER TWENTY-ONE

THE SHOOTING REMAINED constant and heated, and Stillman and Jody headed for its source through several ravines and across a wide park descending toward the Missouri. They knew they were getting close when they heard the Bar 7 men yelling to each other and the whacks and whines of the slugs.

Stillman and Jody tied their horses to cottonwoods and climbed a butte. Peering through a notch in the butte top, Stillman peered across the sagey flat below. Shambeau's Sharps buffalo rifle exploded and puffed smoke high up on another butte, in a nest of rocks from which the split stump of an old cottonwood protruded.

On Stillman's right were two Bar 7 men. Shambeau had them trapped in a small stable partially dug out of a brushy knoll. The knoll was behind the men who hunkered behind their dead horses in the makeshift corral. A third man—Avery Wilkinson, it appeared—lay dead just outside the split cottonwood logs of the corral fence. Blood shone in a gaping wound between his shoulder blades.

Looking farther west, Stillman saw an adobe and log cabin with a sod roof. Apparently, the Bar 7 men had been about to hole up in the cabin for the night.

Stillman winced and shook his head. They never should have tried it. The cabin no doubt belonged to Shambeau. The trapper had probably led them right to it, hoping they'd do just what they'd done.

"Well, he has them now," Stillman said to Jody, hunkered beside him. The shooting below made an angry din. Shambeau's Sharps sounded like field artillery, exploding about once every fifteen seconds, the heavy slugs plunking into the dead horses, jostling them slightly and making the two men— Falk and Milt Polly—cower like thieves.

Jody said, "Try to sneak around behind him?"

Stillman surveyed his surroundings, trying to find a way they could creep around and get on the river side of the trapper.

"Might have to wait till the sun goes down," he said. "It's pretty open down there. We could ride farther west, then circle back, but—"

He stopped when he spied movement in the corral. Falk and Polly had stood, firing their revolvers. They ran, shuffling sideways and shooting, to the cabin side of the corral. They ducked through the logs and, as Shambeau's heavy rifle kicked up dirt around them and blew widgets from the corral, they ran, returning fire, toward the cabin.

Falk paused outside the front door and raised his gun to fire. When the hammer clicked on an empty chamber, the kid cursed and pushed through the plank door. Polly was close on his heels. Shambeau's rifle exploded, and Polly gave a yell as his right leg buckled beneath him. Falk turned, pulled Polly through the door, and slammed the door behind them.

"Stupid devils," Jody breathed.

"Yeah, they're like rats in a cage now ... unless, like you said, we can work around behind him."

"By the time we did that, though," Jody said, glancing at the sun, "it might be dark."

Stillman nodded. "And he might have moved by then, too." He thought about it, sliding his eyes between the trapper's nest of rocks and the cabin. The shooting had stopped, and an eerie quiet had settled into the canyon. "We may be better wait right here for him to show himself. As long as he doesn't know we're here, he might do just that."

"After dark?"

"Probably closer to morning, when the two in the cabin have had ample chance to get good and squirrely."

Stillman tapped Jody's shoulder, and they both slid back behind the brow of the butte, hidden from view. Stillman removed his hat and ran his hands through his thick hair, adjusting the bandage.

"How's your noggin?" Jody asked.

"A mite tender."

"You really ought to see a doc about that."

"Well, in case you hadn't noticed, we're about a three-day ride from a sawbones. I'll live."

Jody studied him and smiled wanly. "Sometimes I'd swear you was Pa come to life again."

"Well, we were together a long time, me and Milk River Bill. He was the first friend I had when I came west after the war, and we stuck together through thick and thin. I reckon some of each of us rubbed off on the other." Stillman squinted his eyes at Jody and inclined his head. "I know a lot of him rubbed off on you. And that ain't necessarily a compliment."

Jody grinned, knowing it was.

"You think we'll take him alive?" he asked after a thoughtful silence.

"Shambeau?" Stillman rested his wrists on his up-raised knees and thought it over, his thick hair ruffling in the breeze which cooled now as the sun sank. Toward the river Canada geese honked and quarreled. He turned to Jody. "*If* we can take him, I guess *how* we'll take him will be up to him."

"You ever run into anyone like him before?"

"Hell, I used to ride with 'em," Stillman said. He picked up a pebble and flung it side-armed down the butte. "Never had to hunt one, though. Feels funny, like I'm hunting one of my own."

They sat listening for sounds, then Stillman turned to where the horses were tied to the cottonwoods. "Maybe you better move the horses back a ways behind that next butte north there. I'll stay here and keep an eye on Shambeau."

"You got it," Jody said, stealing off down the slope while Stillman turned and peered through the notch in the butte top.

All was quiet. There was no sign of movement

When would the trapper make his move? Would he wait for good dark? Or maybe he'd wait until the Bar 7 men had rattled around in their cage for a few hours and jump them at first light tomorrow morning.

All Stillman knew for sure was that Shambeau had all the time in the world. The two men in the cabin were probably dangerously low on food and ammunition.

Several hours passed.

"Ben, I heard something."

Stillman opened his eyes, coming instantly awake. He'd dozed off after Jody had started his second watch. The sky was full of stars but faintly paling in the east

"What is it?"

"Something's moving down there, around the cabin."

Stillman scampered to peer through the notch. He scoured the valley for a full minute. Then he donned his hat and picked up his rifle. "Let's go," he whispered, moving westward along the butte, staying just below the ridgeline.

They descended the butte, stepping carefully around rocks and tree roots and came upon the corral from the east side, with the corral between them and the cabin. They hunkered down behind the knoll from which the stable had been dug, and Stillman scanned the terrain around them.

The dawn light had not yet penetrated the ravine, and all was dark. The ravine was still, as was the cabin. The men inside had had the good sense not to build a fire or light a lamp. Stiilman hadn't heard a peep from either of them all night long. Apparently, Jody hadn't, either.

All was quiet, but what was the sound Jody had heard?

An animal of some kind? Or Shambeau making his move on the cabin?

The tightening of the hair on Stillman's neck told him the latter.

He heard something. It sounded like a low grumble. He heard it again, but it was louder this time—a man's voice raised in question.

Something thumped in the cabin and a man yelled, "Oh! Oh! Oh, no! Oh ... ah ... *Jeee-sus!*"

Stillman turned to Jody. "He must be in the cabin. You stay here."

Then he turned and ran. As he came around the front of the corral, a rifle barked. Stillman had seen the gun flash on the cabin roof. He ducked behind the corral and raised his rifle as the gunman fired again.

Stiilman heard a cry behind him. Turning to his right, he saw the silhouette of Jody on his knees, clutching his bowed head with both hands.

"I told you to stay put, damnit! You all right?"

"He just grazed my forehead," Jody said as he crawled behind a corral post.

Stillman raised his rifle again to the roof and fired, but he couldn't see what he was shooting at. The cabin door opened and the two Bar 7 men ran out, yelling and screaming as though witches were on their heels. The gun on the roof barked again, but this time the flash was directed at the men who'd run out of the cabin.

Stillman lifted the Henry and fired three quick rounds at the cabin roof, but again, he couldn't see what he was shooting at. He waited for more flashes from Shambeau's Sharps, but when none came, he called, "Falk! Polly!"

Several seconds passed before a thin, weak voice said, "It's ... Falk. Milt's dead." Stiilman looked around, trying to pick him out of the darkness. Then he saw a shadow move up close to the cabin, near the front door, where the kid must have moved to escape Shambeau's rifle.

"Where's the trapper?"

"On the roof." The kid's voice was strained, but it rose several octaves as he said, "He dropped snakes—*diamondbacks*—down the chimney pipe!"

A pistol barked three times. *Pow! Pow! Pow!*

"Falk?"

"What?"

"What're you shootin' at?" Stillman asked.

"One of them damn sons o' devils slithered out the damn door!"

Stillman looked around, breathing shallowly so he could hear. The dawn was quiet, lightening gradually, with a breath of breeze ruffling the dew-damp grass. The stars faded. Far off, in the northern buttes, an owl called.

Stillman heard the kid whimpering almost inaudibly.

"Falk?"

"What?"

"What's the matter?"

"I'm gonna die."

Stillman licked his lips and fingered his Henry's trigger. "What makes you say that?"

"'Cause that son of a duck's comin' for me. I can hear him.

He's moving around the side of the cabin." He gave a cry and sniffed. "And... I'm all out of shells."

"Run, damnit!"

The kid's voice was shrill with fear and outrage. "I'm snakebit! My ankle's swollen up like a—"

To the kid's right, a rifle flashed and barked. Stillman brought the butt of the Henry to his cheek and fired, jacking quickly, until six empty cartridges lay around him in the grass. He lowered the rifle, seeing nothing but the vague outline of the cabin against the slowly blanching sky.

He called, "Kid?"

No answer.

Stillman turned to his right. "Jody?"

"I'm all right."

"Stay where you are, and stay alert, understand?"

Jody said he did, and Stillman fired another shot at the cabin, then ran to the cabin and pressed his back against the wall facing the corral. He shuffled sideways to the front, paused, then jerked around the corner and peered through the softening darkness before him, his finger on the Henry's trigger.

Nothing moved.

He moved forward, ducking under a window, then stumbled on something and stopped. Keeping his eyes riveted on whatever might lie before him, he crouched down, reaching out and down with his left hand, which came to rest on a man's shoulder.

He lowered his gaze, crouching. It was the kid sitting on his butt with his back against the wall, his head tilted to his shoulder. There was a bloody puddle on his chest. Stillman felt for a pulse, found none.

"Stupid damn ..." he groused, moving on.

He stopped when he heard something. It sounded like a foot lightly crunching grass. His skin rippled with goosebumps as he dropped to his knees. A dark figure jerked around the cabin's far corner. There was a flash and a roar and the instant, rotten-egg smell of burnt powder as the .56-caliber slug whistled over Stillman's head.

The lawman raised the Henry barrel with one hand and fired. He heard a grunt and the clatter of a rifle hitting the ground. Shambeau jerked back behind the cabin, and Stillman heard footfalls.

Jumping to his feet, he ran to the corner and stopped, looking back along the cabin. Something moved to his left. Swinging his gaze that way, he saw the trapper running toward the buttes silhouetted against the sky. Standing the Henry along the cabin wall, Stillman took off, running hard through a clearing and then through a Cottonwood copse, hurdling a deadfall and several branches.

He came to a cut in the buttes and, drawing his revolver, walked slowly through to a deep-cut bank. Stillman crept to the edge of the bank and looked down.

Thirty feet below lay a bend of the wide, flat Missouri, milky brown in the dawn light. On the far, rocky shore, a flock of Canada geese lifted, honking and flapping their wings. The water smelled clean and cold with mountain snowmelt.

Stillman heard a rock tumbling behind him. He whipped around, his breath catching in his throat. Before him, the trapper stood on a ledge in the butte face. He crouched, hands on his knees, breathing hard. He looked exhausted. His face was pale and hollow, and he appeared at least ten years older than the last time Stillman had seen him.

There was a bloody hole in his wolf coat, to the right of his heart. In his right hand a knife blade flashed.

Stillman clicked back his Colt's hammer. "It's all over, Louis. Give it up."

The trapper glared at him, his broad chest rising and falling as he breathed. He looked like an old grizzly run to ground by a pack of hungry wolves—utterly spent but defiant to the end.

Stillman reached into his coat pocket with his free hand and brought out a pair of manacles. Underhanded, he tossed them onto the ledge. "Put those on, Louis, and we'll get the hell out of here."

Shambeau looked at the manacles at his feet then lifted his eyes again to Stillman. He shook his head.

"Lawman," he said, wrinkling his nose distastefully.

Suddenly he flicked the knife in the air and caught it with his right hand, making a savage fist. Then, drawing his lips back from his teeth and howling like a warlock, he sprang off the ledge toward Stillman.

Stillman fired two quick shots and hurled himself sideways, out of the trapper's path. Hitting the ground on his right shoulder, Stillman turned sharply to see Shambeau's moccasined feet disappear over the cutbank. A half second later, a thunderous splash lifted from the river.

Stillman pushed himself to his feet and peered into the frothing, rippling water. Shambeau's head and shoulders appeared at the center of a boiling circle, the trapper's hair plastered to his scalp, his beard flat against his cheeks. His eyes were gently closed, and the expression on his face appeared strangely serene.

He turned slowly in the gray water bubbling blood, and then his face inclined. His arms rose as if surrendering to the current, which tugged him resolutely downstream and out of sight around a bend.

Stillman stood for a long time on the high bank, unable to believe the chase was finally over, incredulous that he'd brought the mountain man down with mere bullets.

The man was only human, after all.

Stillman sighed, sleeved sweat from his forehead, and holstered his revolver.

Feeling old—as old as the dying stars and the river muttering behind him—he started back toward the cabin.

High above, in a sky lanced with the first yellow spears of the rising sun, the geese barked and honked, heading for the mountain parks for breakfast.

CHAPTER TWENTY-TWO

IT WAS PULLING on toward late in the afternoon, and the traffic on First Street was dwindling.

Getting a leg up on their closing preparations, several shopkeepers were sweeping the boardwalks in front of their establishments. A few others stood outside reading the paper and smoking, soaking up the warm sunlight, still a novelty after the long northern winter, before it was gone for the day.

Dogs had awakened from afternoon naps to prowl, and hired boys split cordwood in paper-littered alleys choked with barrels and shipping crates. Sam Wa, returning from a bath at Albright's bathhouse, hailed the new blacksmith, Gunner Dugan, and turned into his café to prepare for the Thursday night supper crowd.

Feeling even more refreshed than Sam Wa, Blade Carstairs stepped out of Serena's First Avenue Pleasure Palace, a crisp, new *Bugle* under his arm. He straightened his string tie, jerked at the lapels of his Prince Albert coat, and adjusted the black, flat-brimmed hat upon his head, his wavy hair still damp from the bath he'd taken with one of Serena's pleasure girls, and gave it a slightly rakish tip over his right eye. Then he turned right and headed south toward First Street— every inch the proud, determined businessman with little but good, honest commerce on his mind.

When he came to First Street, he turned left and strolled along the boardwalk, greeting shoppers and shopkeepers as he passed. At the corner of First Street and Second Avenue, he paused at an awning post, removed his watch from his pocket, and flipped the lid.

Just about time.

He waited, scanning the front page of the freshly printed paper and hearing the proprietor of the tinware shop whistling as he swept dust and cigarette butts from the boardwalk before his window. Shortly, Carstairs heard boots thump, and turned to see Calvin Whitehead strolling up the boardwalk along Second Avenue, wearing a long, cream duster which only partially concealed the shotgun hanging from a leather lanyard around his neck.

When Whitehead stopped beside him, Carstairs turned to Sam Wa's Cafe as the front door opened. Evelyn Vincent appeared in the open door, looking as scrumptious as ever in a low-cut blue dress, a blue ribbon in her curly blond hair. She paused in the open door and glanced at Carstairs and Whitehead.

Blade flashed a reassuring smile and touched the brim of his hat. He couldn't wait to get into that girl's drawers. Shouldn't be long now ...

Evelyn nodded in greeting, stepped onto the boardwalk, and, lifting her skirts above the dust and horse dung, headed across the street toward the jailhouse.

When she made the awning outside the jail, Carstairs turned his gaze back to the other side of the street. Big Newt Jarvis stepped out from the gap between the harness shop and the dentist's office. He, too, wore a long, cream duster. He puffed a thick stogie and looked as ridiculous as ever in his broadcloth trousers and bowler hat. He did a good imitation of an ape, Blade thought, all gussied up for a Sunday church meeting.

Carstairs elbowed Whitehead, and the two men started across Second Avenue, past the feed store and an open lot. As they passed before the jail, they slowed slightly, hearing Evelyn giggling and the deputy chuckling behind the dusty window. When they'd passed the jail, Carstairs turned to Whitehead with a grin and a wink.

"Didn't I tell you that girl would earn her keep?"

Whitehead chuckled dryly and gave a reluctant nod. "I still say she's gonna be trouble down the line."

"You think all women are trouble down the line, Cal."

"That's 'cause they are!" Whitehead insisted.

"Easy, easy. I don't intend on lettin' her follow us." A devilish grin played across his face. "Not for more than a few nights, anyway."

Whitehead chuckling dryly and, shaking his head, they continued past Harrison's Grocery and Drug Store then paused on the corner of Third Avenue. Carstairs glanced at Newt Jarvis standing directly across the street, his back to the dentist's office, waiting.

Blade gave him the signal that everything was a go— a wide yawn behind his open hand. Then he and Whitehead started walking catty-corner across First Street and Third Avenue, toward the Stockmen's Bank and Trust. They met Jarvis along the building's east wall and stood as if in friendly conversation as they glanced around to see if they were being watched.

When he was certain none of the few people on the street suspected their intentions, Carstairs took one more gander at the jail, where Evelyn was entertaining the deputy. Then he turned, walked around the corner of the building, and strolled casually through the bank's front door, Jarvis and Whitehead following.

"All right, this is a holdup!" he yelled, drawing his revolver and flashing it at the teller in his cage and at the bank president seated at his desk behind the mahogany rail. "*Mi amigos* will supply the sacks. All you have to do is fill them with greenbacks!"

Jarvis pushed past the three customers who had been waiting in line at the Paying and Receiving window, and Whitehead hurdled the rail.

"On your feet and in the vault," he told the president, a stocky man in a gray suit and gold-rimmed spectacles. "Now! Move!"

"Just sit tight there, my good man," Carstairs told the loan clerk, a young, mustached gent who sat at a rolltop desk facing the wall. He appeared fidgety and cunning, and Carstairs didn't like either trait in those he was robbing. They were likely to pull a derringer or some other hideout from the end of a watch chain or some sleeve contraption.

The three people who'd been standing in line appeared relatively calm. They stood to the left of Carstairs, their hands raised—an old lady in a blue calico housedress, a farmer in a bullet-crowned hat and Quaker beard, and a plain young woman wearing the dour, spiritless expression of a store-clerk's wife.

Carstairs covered them and the clerk, swinging his gun from left to right, staying back by the wall. Jarvis was yelling at the teller to hurry, and, back in the vault, Whitehead was doing the same to the president, using just enough epithets to make the women blush and the farmer to wrinkle his nose uncomfortably.

"You'll never get away with this," the clerk said, sitting on his swivel chair, his small, beringed hands in the air.

"Shut up," Carstairs said. "And empty your pockets on the desk."

The clerk's face blanched. "What? I—"

"You heard me," Blade said, aiming his revolver at the clerk and ratcheting back the hammer. "Empty your damn pockets, smartass!"

When the clerk had done as ordered, Carstairs told him to remove his rings, as well. The man looked truly pained by the order, but, with Carstairs's weapon aimed directly at his left eye, he complied, wrapping everything in the top page of his blotter, and giving it a halfhearted toss to Carstairs, who caught it with a grin and a wink.

By this time, Jarvis had two sacks filled with greenbacks

and was waiting by the door, peering anxiously out at the street. "Come on, Cal—what's takin' so damn long?" he yelled at the vault.

The only answer was more epithets spewed at the president. A minute later Whitehead appeared holding two hefty bags in each hand. He whooped and said, "Much obliged, Mr. Fancy-Pants!" He kicked the heavy door closed, locking the president inside, then came running, tossing two bags over the rail. Carstairs caught them, nearly dropping them as he laughed at their weight

"There was more cash back there than we even figured!" Whitehead whooped.

"Come on, come on," Jarvis carped from the door. "I'm gettin' nervous. It's too damn quiet out there."

"Take it easy, Newt," Blade said, adjusting the bags in his arms. Turning to the teller and the clerk, he said, "Much obliged, good people. Keep up the good work, and maybe we'll see ye again real soon!"

With that he turned and headed out the door, which Newt Jarvis had already opened. On the boardwalk he hung a sharp right heading down Third Avenue toward the alley flanking the bank. He ran as fast as he could with the heavy bags, laughing, the other two men following close behind.

Jarvis mumbled, "I got a funny feelin' about this, dammit!"

"Oh, take it easy, Jarvis," Calvin Whitehead said, his voice trilling as he ran. "You're rich, for chrissakes!"

"Wait a minute," Blade said. He'd just turned into the alley and, seeing the empty hitchrack behind the bank, stopped suddenly. The others did likewise. "Where are the horses, Jarvis?"

"I tied 'em right there!"

"Are you sure it was here?" Whitehead snarled.

"Of course I'm sure."

There was a two-hole privy on their left, about twenty feet away. The privy door squeaked.

"Hold it right there, boys," Leon McMannigle said.

He'd been waiting in the privy. Now he stepped out, his long-barreled Smith & Wesson extended in his right hand, hammer back. A second revolver, an old model Colt, was wedged behind his cartridge belt, the butt against his belly.

"One move and they'll be putting you to bed with picks and shovels."

"What the hell?" Carstairs rasped, turning his head slightly to see the deputy over his shoulder.

"You done been duped and duped good," Leon said, a touch of humor in his deep, sonorous voice. "Now drop them guns."

"By the girl?" Jarvis asked.

"I ain't gonna tell you again. I want all your hardware on the ground. Now!"

"Damn you, Blade!" Whitehead shouted. "I told you she was no good!"

Carstairs just stood there, his face flushed, his jaw set hard. He couldn't quite believe what had happened. He'd always been able to sweet-talk women onto his side without any trouble at all. Women loved him. Why, when they gazed at Blade Carstairs, they had stars in their eyes!

Damn—women were crazy for him!

Damn—women would give him the shirts off their backs ... the shoes off their feet... !

"That devil!" he said.

"Drop it, Carstairs. You too, Jarvis. Whitehead."

"That devil done sold us out!" Jarvis carped at Carstairs.

"Drop 'em!"

There was a tense pause, the three robbers standing before Leon stiffly, their guns in one hand, money sacks in the other.

"Well, I don't know about you fellas," Jarvis seethed, dropping his money sack, "but I ain't lettin' no deputy nigger take me in!"

He jerked around, bringing his shotgun up. Before the barrel was level, however, Leon fired a bullet through his chest, knocking him backward off his feet. Jarvis hadn't landed before Carstairs brought his own gun to bear, raging, "Damn you to hell!"

Leon fired again, aiming at the sunlight flashing on Carstairs's Colt. The bullet smashed through Blade's hand, drilling a neat little hole about an inch below the middle knuckle, and pinged against his Colt, throwing it wide.

Carstairs screamed, clutching the wounded limb, squeezing it between his knees.

Leon brought his revolver to bear on Whitehead, who had started turning toward him, but froze when he'd seen his compatriots go down. He dropped his shotgun and money sack quickly, throwing his hands up and lacing them behind his head. "Don't shoot!"

"Now, that's what I like to hear," Leon said, moving forward.

Gun extended, he patted down Carstairs as he stood holding his wounded hand, grunting and cursing. When he'd discarded the ringleader's two hideout guns, he handcuffed him, then patted down Whitehead and cuffed him, as well. He could tell without even having to check for a pulse that Jarvis was dead.

"I need a doctor, damnit!" Carstairs raged, his crimson face creased with pain.

"You'll get one soon enough," Leon said, pushing him and Whitehead toward the street

Footsteps sounded on the boardwalk, and then the bank president and his loan clerk appeared around the corner, running into the alley. "You got 'em!" the president yelled. "Good work, Leon!"

"Anyone hurt inside?"

"No one," the clerk said as he followed the president after the money, some of which had seeped out one of the sacks and was blowing westward down the alley. "We all stayed calm, just like you said, Leon."

"Good for you," McMannigle said, and pushed the two men into the street.

As they started down Third Avenue, toward the jail, Doc Evans and Evelyn Vincent ran toward them. Evans carried his stout, double-barreled greener in case Leon had needed any help. "Leon, you got 'em!" Evelyn cried. "Thank God!"

"You devil!" Carstairs raged.

"That's no way to talk to a lady," Evans said with a touch of irony.

"She's no lady," Carstairs groused, twisting the wrist of his injured hand.

"Well, you're no gentleman!" Evelyn shot back, fists on her hips.

Whitehead turned to Evans. "That was you in the jail ...with her?"

"Laughing, you mean?" Evans grinned. "Yes, that was me." He put his arm around Evelyn's shoulders. "We were having a little laugh over your pictures on the Wanted posters Leon found in his desk drawer. You boys didn't even have the sense to change your names!"

Evelyn giggled. Producing a long slip of paper from the bosom of her dress, she said, "Here's your stage ticket, Blade. I guess I won't be needing it after all. But thanks, anyway." She laughed.

Carstairs took the ticket, scowling, and tossed it into the wind. He cursed and turned to the deputy. "Are we going to stand here all night? I'm bleeding to death!"

"Doc, will you look at his hand for him? It's all shot to hell."

"Yeah, I'll have a look at it after supper," Evans said as he and Evelyn started for Sam Wa's.

"Hey, what about my damn hand?" Blade fumed.

Leon pushed him and the thoroughly cowed Whitehead toward the jailhouse. "You heard the doc. He'll have a look at it after supper." Leon chuckled. "If he ain't half shot by then."

EPILOGUE

TWO DAYS LATER Leon and Doc Evans were sitting outside the jail, in the shade beneath the awning. They had their legs crossed, and they were smoking the tobacco which the doctor had ordered in special from St. Louis. It was a dark Turkish blend, finely cut, and it smelled sweet and aromatic.

Not only that, but it seemed to burn especially slow—or did the slow burning result from the fine-grained, tissue-thin paper the doctor had also ordered?

It had been a slow, warm, summery morning, and they were discussing the merits of the cigarettes, studying their ashes, when Leon glanced up to see a grizzled man in a cream-colored, high-crowned, Texas-style hat riding along First Street on a bay horse that looked a hell of a lot like Sweets.

Leon stared at the trail-worn figure, scrutinizing the broad-shouldered man beneath all that dust and sweat and several days worth of beard on his jaw. A buckskin coat was tied behind the man's saddle, and he wore a blue-checked flannel shirt with the sleeves rolled above his elbows. The man's forearms were tanned and corded with muscle, slick with sweat. Evans stopped talking when he saw that Leon's attention had been compromised. Turning to see what the deputy was gawking at, he, too frowned, and exhaled a slow, thin stream of smoke from his nose and mouth.

"Why, that's Ben."

Leon stood. "I'll be damned." He grinned. "It is!"

He ran into the street as Stillman drew near, heavy and slouched in his saddle. "Ben—hellfire and damnation! It's you! You been gone over a week! We 'bout gave up on you! What the hell happened, anyway? Where's Jody? What about Shambeau?"

The deputy sidled up to Stillman's stirrup as the sheriff drew up to the hitchrack. He didn't have to rein Sweets to a halt. The horse knew he was home, and his tired rump rippled with mute delight.

"Jody went on home," Stillman said tiredly. "Shambeau's dead. The Bar Seven men are dead. It's over. Finished. Done with."

"The Bar Seven men?" Leon asked, frowning.

"It's a long story," Stillman said. "I'll tell you all about it as soon as I get a bath and about a week's worth of shut-eye." He groaned as he not so much dismounted as rolled out of his saddle.

"Will you pull the gear off ole Sweets for me and stable him with plenty of oats and water?" he asked the deputy.

"And I'll give him one hell of a rubdown," Leon said, grabbing Sweets's bridle. "Looks like he needs it."

"We both do," Stillman said. "I'm gonna go home and get mine from a schoolteacher I know."

"She's been in every day lookin' for you," Leon said, taking the bay's reins. "She'll be at school now, though."

"I'm gonna climb into a hot tub and wait for her."

Like a man half asleep, Stillman shucked his Henry from his saddle boot and started walking toward French Street, kneading the back of his neck with his right hand.

"Oh," he said, turning to Leon and Evans, who stood watching him wistfully. "Anything happen around here while I was gone?"

Leon bit his lip and furled his brow, studying his boots thoughtfully. "Uh... let me see." He glanced at Evans. "Can you think of anything, Doc?"

Evans shrugged. "No, it's been pretty quiet around here, Ben. I set a few broken bones. Mrs. Lotton's water broke a few hours ago. Katherine's with her now." He shrugged again and glanced at Leon. "That's about it."

"Yeah, it's been pretty quiet, Ben. You know—calving season and all. You go on home and get some rest."

Stillman nodded gratefully. "I think I'll do that."

He turned and ambled down the boardwalk.

McMannigle looked at Evans, a devilish smile toying with the deputy's lips, and drew deep on his cigarette.

A LOOK AT: Once Upon A Dead Man

(Sheriff Ben Stillman Book 7)

A MURDERED LAWMAN AND A FRONTIER TOWN WITH A DEADLY SECRET...

Sheriff Ben Stillman knows that every lawman could face sudden death. But that doesn't ease his anger over Marshal Charlie Boomhauer's brutal murder. And ol' Charlie's shoes have already been filled by his brash, young deputy—who isn't exactly out shaking the bushes to find Charlie's killer or killers.

The new marshal is blaming the murder on a band of Gypsies who moved north—or was it south? It's becoming clear that the town of Lone Pine has something to hide—and that Stillman is outside his jurisdiction. But the lawman's code says that you take care of your own. Ben isn't going home until he's served up some justice—whether it's by the rules or not.

Once Upon a Dead Man is seventh novel in the fast-moving, western classic Sheriff Ben Stillman Series.

AVAILABLE MAY 2019 FROM PETER BRANDVOLD AND WOLFPACK PUBLISHING

ABOUT THE AUTHOR

Peter Brandvold grew up in the great state of North Dakota in the 1960's and '70s, when television westerns were as popular as shows about hoarders and shark tanks are now, and western paperbacks were as popular as Game of Thrones.

Brandvold watched every western series on television at the time. He grew up riding horses and herding cows on the farms of his grandfather and many friends who owned livestock.

Brandvold's imagination has always lived and will always live in the West. He is the author of over a hundred lightning-fast action westerns under his own name and his pen name, Frank Leslie.

READ MORE ABOUT PETER BRANDVOLD HERE:
https://wolfpackpublishing.com/peter-brandvold/

CPSIA information can be obtained
at www.ICGtesting.com
Printed in the USA
LVHW040122150819
627731LV00002B/153/P